Passion's
FOUR TOWERS

DEE BRICE

ELLORA'S CAVE
ROMANTICA PUBLISHING

An Ellora's Cave Romantica Publication

www.ellorascave.com

Passion's Four Towers

ISBN 9781419956706
ALL RIGHTS RESERVED.
Passion's Four Towers Copyright © 2007 Dee Brice
Edited by Helen Woodall
Cover art by Philip Fuller

Electronic book Publication March 2007
Trade paperback Publication June 2007

Excerpt from *Sword and Crown* Copyright © Lauren Dane, 2007

This book printed in the U.S.A. by Jasmine-Jade Enterprises, LLC.

Content Advisory:

S – ENSUOUS
E – ROTIC
X – TREME

Ellora's Cave Publishing offers three levels of Romantica™ reading entertainment: S (S-ensuous), E (E-rotic), and X (X-treme).

The following material contains graphic sexual content meant for mature readers. This story has been rated E–rotic.

S-*ensuous* love scenes are explicit and leave nothing to the imagination.

E-*rotic* love scenes are explicit, leave nothing to the imagination, and are high in volume per the overall word count. E-rated titles might contain material that some readers find objectionable—in other words, almost anything goes, sexually. E-rated titles are the most graphic titles we carry in terms of both sexual language and descriptiveness in these works of literature.

X-*treme* titles differ from E-rated titles only in plot premise and storyline execution. Stories designated with the letter X tend to contain difficult or controversial subject matter not for the faint of heart.

About the Author

৪৩

Dee believes she was born with a pen in one hand and a writing tablet in the other. Determined not to work in an office, this wannabe actress never learned to type well; she still composes with pen and pad, then transcribes her manuscripts onto her PC. Sometimes Dee and her dictation program are best friends; more often they are mortal enemies.

Dee lives in northern California with her inspiration, best friend, and husband. She loves to read and, of course, write. Passion's Four Towers is her first published novel.

Dee welcomes comments from readers. You can find her website and email address on her author bio page at www.ellorascave.com.

Tell Us What You Think

We appreciate hearing reader opinions about our books. You can email us at Comments@EllorasCave.com.

PASSION'S FOUR TOWERS

లు

Dedication

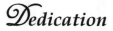

Dedicated to Himself: My best friend, my inspiration, my mate.

Prologue

ဆ

I, Kerrie, Queen of Marchonland, being of sound mind…

"Alexandre, stop it!" Kerrie said, laughing. Her husband's tongue lapping at her neck tickled and made her nipples pucker with desire. But as a new mother and a queen, she had an obligation to complete her will.

"Come to bed, Kerrie, while our babe still sleeps."

"Only half an hour more, Alexandre. I promise."

Grumbling good-naturedly under his breath, he retreated to their bed.

Kerrie retrieved her quill and continued to write. After a time she finished with, *When she comes of age, Yvonne is to marry the heir to Puttupon. This is my wish and that of Yvonne's father and the heir's parents.*

Placing her signature and seal on the parchment, she rushed to the bed. Discarding her gown, shivering, she climbed in bed beside her husband.

And found Alexandre dead.

Three years later Kerrie added to her will.

When Willa and Yvonne reach maturity, Yvonne will marry the Puttupon heir and Willa will marry as my husband and I determine. Brecc's only stipulation is that our daughter's husband be of noble birth.

"Come to bed, dearling, or I'll start without you."

"Only a moment longer, sweet Brecc. I must check on our daughter."

Kerrie retreated to the nursery and bestowed a kiss on each of her daughters' brows. Returning to her bedchamber, she skimmed off her night rail and eased beneath the covers.

"Poor Brecc. Did you miss me so much you grew cold from waiting?" She kissed his cheek and ran her hand down his chest to the juncture of his thighs. There, his cock was limp, his cum still warm upon the cold hand that gripped it.

Two years later Kerrie affixed her seal to her amended will and signed it.

When Pippa reaches maturity she, Willa and Yvonne will marry according to my previous instructions. Cesare, Pippa's father, asks only that she find passion before she weds so that she will know the happiness Cesare and I have shared. So I wish for all my daughters.

"Cesare, sweeting, wrap me in your hair and warm me."

"Mount me, Kerrie. Take my *bacamarte* into you and milk me."

She did and their cries of completion mingled. She collapsed against his chest and wept when he sighed her name and breathed no more.

One year later Kerrie signed her name to the last letter she would ever write.

Aida — Dearest Sister,

Today D asked me to marry him. He wants to give me sons — sons! — to rule Marchonland. I haven't told him that not only will a man never rule my country, but that I can no longer give any man a child. D thinks my lack of menses these last two months is because I already am breeding, carrying his babe — his son!

I know I am young, yet I also know I shall never bear another child. Nor shall I marry again.

Take care of my (here she struck through *my*) *our daughters. Tell them every day how much I love them.*

She added a postscript beneath her signature.

And if their husbands die before they do, advise them not to marry again. No one should have to bury the love of her life more than once.

Chapter One

ကာ

"Dehy's following us again," Yvonne said as she and her two sisters left Marchon Castle behind and trekked toward the apple orchard.

Pippa frowned. "I can't see the pest. Can you, Willa?"

"No, but I don't have Yvonne's keen eyes," Willa said.

"Take heart, Pippa. He's only following us because Willa's with us. Perhaps we should go to our swimming hole." Yvonne's voice held laughter but her expression was somber.

"Don't start," Willa said, her voice menacing, a smile curving her lips.

"Yes, let's go for a swim. Willa can disrobe as she did last summer, slowly, inch-by-inch revealing her body. And you and I, Yvonne, can eavesdrop on Dehy when he tells the stable boys whether he likes Willa's plump handfuls and ass as much as he did last year."

"Pfft!" Willa spat then grinned at her siblings. "Keep on teasing and I'll order Cook to feed you only the most fattening foods." She sighed. "Not that it would do much good with all the exercise you two get."

"There's not much difference among us," Yvonne said, grasping her sisters' hands. "Walking the fields with Gaspar keeps you slim, Willa."

"Compared to you and Pippa, I'm fat."

"Pfft!" her sisters said together.

"Besides," Willa continued, "if we want our conversation to remain private, the orchard is the best place for it. Dehy won't come anywhere near the mother tree."

"Nor will any of the stable boys," Pippa said. "Do either of you know why?"

Willa shook her head, but Yvonne nodded. "Poor superstitious darlings. They all believe our mother tree grew the very apple that Eve used to tempt Adam."

"I think it was the snake that tempted Eve," Willa said.

"Whatever," Pippa said, waving her free hand dismissively. "Men blame women for every misfortune that befalls them."

Willa and Yvonne muttered their agreement.

"Perhaps Willa should take Dehy to her bed. 'Twould save us the trouble of this miserable tournament Aunt Aida and Gaspar are planning," Yvonne said, only half joking.

"Dehy is a child."

"Eighteen to your twenty," Pippa said.

"And besides, the tournament was neither Aunt Aida's nor Gaspar's idea."

"No," Pippa agreed, "it was our wretched—"

Willa and Yvonne gasped, appalled that Pippa would speak ill of the dead.

"Our mother's idea, may she rest in peace," Pippa corrected, her voice bitter. She'd heard enough gossip about her mother's love of men to think Kerrie uninvolved with her daughters' present predicament.

They walked on in silence until they reached the orchard and the mother tree. Spreading their cloaks on the ground, they brought out their supplies and ate.

Willa passed out chunks of cheese and accepted bread from Yvonne and a winter apple from Pippa.

13

"Perhaps," Pippa said, "we could choose another suitor for Willa. Someone older, someone she knows and respects."

"Gaspar!" Yvonne crowed.

"He won't accept. Besides Aunt Aida would kill us all," Pippa said, looking at Yvonne as if she'd lost her mind. "They've been lovers since dirt was a baby."

"It wouldn't have to be real," Yvonne said in a reasonable tone. "Gaspar could make Aunt Aida see reason and—"

"No," Willa said so firmly her sisters gaped at her.

"Leave Gaspar out of this," Pippa admonished. "Now, Yvonne, since you are the oldest, you have—"

"Right of first refusal. I claim it. I refuse to have any part in saving us all from marriage."

"An obligation to Willa and to me to make the sacrifice."

"But I am the defender of Marchon Castle! Who will defend us if I marry and go live who knows where? Will you, Pippa?"

Willa broke into the escalating argument. "Pippa is almost as strong as you are, Yvonne, and could learn to defend us. But she plays as important a part in Marchonland's wellbeing as you do. As guardian of the horses—drays for our fields, destriers for our knights, ponies for our peoples' children—she could not easily be replaced either.

"No, Mother's will aside, I must be the one. I am resigned to it. Gaspar is more than capable of carrying out my duties. After all, he did them for years while I was growing up and learning everything I needed to know."

They fell into morose silence.

Willa gazed up at the limbs of the mother tree. Mild March temperatures had tempted new leaves to sprout. Now, in April, pink and white blossoms began to spread their sweet scent over the orchard. Soon Willa would need to lay bouquets of those blossoms at the bases of some of the trees or they would not bear fruit. Unless the bees finally awoke from their winter slumbers and pollinated these trees.

"Pfft!" Yvonne said in disgust several moments later. "Dehy's at it again."

"At what again?"

"You know," Pippa said, pantomiming a man touching himself.

"You mean he's jerking his quim-sticker?" Willa said, her face red, her smile wide.

"Where do you hear such words, Willa? Eavesdropping on my stable boys?" Pippa asked, obviously teasing.

"Eavesdropping on my men-at-arms?" asked Yvonne, crossing her arms over her chest and glaring with mock severity at her younger sister.

"No." Willa laughed. "Eavesdropping on Aida and Gaspar."

Yvonne laughed then said, "Remind Portier to make sure Dehy washes before he returns to duty."

"Ugh!" Pippa said, making a face. "I wish your ears weren't so damn keen."

"Ugh?" Willa said. "This from a woman who watches stallions cover mares."

"From a woman who returns from the stables covered in afterbirth?"

Pippa waved her hands dismissively. "It seems more natural when a stallion mounts a mare."

"Trust me, Pippa, if a stallion had hands he'd jerk off too," Yvonne said wryly.

"Then I am very glad my horses have hooves!"

They lapsed once more into silence.

"I have it! The perfect solution to this debacle Maman and Aunt Aida have gotten us into." Looking at her sisters' forlorn faces, Yvonne felt her elation deflate. "Don't you want to hear?"

Willa said in a defeated voice, "We've been at this for so long my brain is seeping out my ears."

Pippa sighed. "If it's another Gaspar… Oh go ahead, Yvonne. Since you're the oldest, we should at least hear you out."

"I'm getting awfully tired of being the 'oldest'," Yvonne snapped.

"Besides, Pippa, Yvonne comes up with good ideas. Sometimes."

"When? When was the last time Yvonne came up with an idea that didn't land us in a manure heap?"

"Never mind then. I only thought you might like dressing up like a knight, Pippa, and showing off your riding skills."

Pippa looked up from regarding her clenched hands. A spark of interest lit her tawny eyes. "What? What, what, what?"

"Here's the plan. Pippa, you enter the tournament, but only in the horsemanship events—the rings and things like that. I shall enter those events that involve swords and battleaxes and archery. Since we are nearly the same height and build and we'll be wearing helmets, no one will know the difference."

Pippa's smile faded. "Except for archery. You cannot wear a helmet and expect to see. And if you can't wear a helm, how can we continue the disguise?"

"Chain mail," Willa said, for the first time that day looking truly cheerful. The sparkle returned to her turquoise eyes. "Your chain mail will cover your hair, Yvonne, and leave your vision clear. And I shall... What shall I do?"

"Sit in the stands and — "

"If you say 'look pretty' I'll dump you both in the moat."

"But you do look— You are— Your beauty aside, Willa, you are the holder of the land. Everything we have, the horses, the men-at-arms, the crops — everything — you embody. The competitors will expect to see you."

"And when Yvonne and I win, you will present one of us with your favor."

"Then Pippa or I will carry you off to the castle to have our wicked way with you." Yvonne waggled her eyebrows and twirled an imaginary mustache.

"You can take months, perhaps even years," Pippa encouraged, "to make your decision as to which of us you want to marry."

"I doubt Aunt Aida will allow much time at all. Speaking of her — "

Yvonne's cat-like green eyes glittered. "I'm sure Gaspar won't mind keeping our nosy aunt busy."

Pippa grinned. "With any luck at all, she won't be able to walk."

"Let alone climb up and down stairs to check on me and my 'suitors'," Willa added, looking resolute. She blushed then covered her mouth with both hands. She didn't know exactly why she should be embarrassed, but she was. The idea of women making love to women or men loving other men seemed very different, especially given Kerrie's appetites for the opposite sex.

"I believe there's more of our mother in Willa than we suspected," Pippa finally said.

"Let's hope not, or she may agree to a veritable parade of men," Yvonne countered.

"Which might be better than sharing a tower with you two for who knows how long. Pippa always smells like horses and hay and worse. And with you about, Yvonne, with all those sharp weapons of yours, I shan't be able to leave my bed for fear of stepping on one of them."

They shared a laugh then sobered.

"What if you fail?" Even to her own ears, Willa's voice sounded timorous.

"We won't fail," Pippa said in a firm voice.

They both looked up at Yvonne. She shrugged. "There are always the gypsies."

All three nodded. Anything, even trekking with a gypsy caravan, was better than marriage to a man who would expect them all to give way to his wishes.

* * * * *

Several days later Aida stood on the battlements, her head resting against Gaspar's shoulder. It was the only place they could gain privacy during the day. If they retired to her tower, the entire castle would suspect they were doing more than just talking.

"You realize, of course," Gaspar said, "the princesses are plotting something."

"Of course." She sighed. "I just wish I knew what those fertile minds are hatching. I have never seen Pippa ride so many hours a day."

"Or Yvonne spend so much time practicing with mace and battleaxe and sword. She all but ignores her bow."

"Yvonne needs no practice with bow and arrow. She is the finest archer in the land."

"As is Pippa our finest rider," Gaspar said, rubbing his chin and looking puzzled.

"These days Willa seems to spend her time watching her sisters' labors."

"When normally she would worry over each grain of wheat and flower bud. She's even curtailed the time she spends with me going over the accounts."

As if with one voice, they sighed. When Yvonne barely avoided her opponent's sword, Aida cringed. Gaspar cursed as Pippa's head nearly struck the iron ring she attempted to catch on her lance. Willa's scream rose to the battlements like a banshee's wail. Nothing the sisters had done before now had disturbed Willa's serenity.

"We have to stop this before they get hurt."

"But how? Yvonne and Pippa are as stubborn as Kerrie, may she rest in peace. And lately Willa seems as restless as my sister was when she had a man on her mind."

"Don't you mean men and 'rest in piece-by-piece', Aida? Weren't Kerrie's thoughts always on men and fuck—fornication?"

His wry tone took away any insult. Besides, Aida knew he spoke the truth. "Can it be so simple? All their restlessness caused merely by thoughts of men?"

"They are ripe for bedding, Aida. In that their mother was wise."

"But to insist they be seduced before they may marry, that seems most unwise. And who knows who will win the tournament? I'll not give any of my nieces to an ancient or sickly man. Although if a man's strong enough to survive the tournament, he most likely will be young and fit."

They looked at each other as the girls' scheme became apparent. The tournament, of course.

"Which of those minxes came up with that idea?" Gaspar wondered then slapped his forehead.

"Yvonne, no doubt. She is the oldest," Aida said, "and the most like her mother in her daring."

"Pippa went along with the plan because?"

"Most probably to prove her skills on horseback."

"But why would sensible Willa agree to such madness?"

They fell silent then Aida suggested, "Perhaps Willa tires of being sensible."

They groaned. For Willa to throw over caution and sensibility was dire indeed.

"What will we do?"

"We'll devise a plan of our own. If nothing else, we'll prove to them that age and experience have much greater chance of success than…"

"Youthful guile?"

"Whatever," Gaspar said, expelling his breath with a huff. "I think we should retire to your tower and consider this most carefully."

"Will we actually plan?" Aida asked, looking up at him from languid gray eyes.

"We do our best thinking when my quim-sticker is buried deep in your quim."

Aida laughed. "The problem, Gaspar, is that you think only of your cock in me."

"Then what do you think about?"

"The same thing. The very same thing."
Still laughing, they left the battlements.

Chapter Two
Aida's Tower

જી

When they reached Aida's quarters, Gaspar hesitated just inside the outer door.

Halfway to her bedchamber Aida paused and turned to look at him. "Bar it," she said, her low voice husky, her gray eyes turning almost black with desire.

"If you untie a single knot," he warned then chuckled. She was bent over, arranging pillows in front of the fire she'd stoked to heat the cool solar. He wanted to lift her skirts and bury himself deep within her warmth, but she deserved better than that. Besides, he was a man now, not a randy youth who thought only of himself and his own pleasure.

"Are you sure you want this?" he said, capturing her hands and drawing her up to face him.

"Yes. I am in desperate need of you." She sank down upon the pillows, drew him down with her.

"I'll not let you rush me." He stilled her questing hands, settled her so her ass rested between his splayed thighs. Laving her ear, he removed the bit of lace covering her hair. She shivered and wiggled her buttocks against his rising erection.

"Won't you?" Her breathless voice challenged his control.

"I won't." He found her first hairpin, removed it then sifted the drooping auburn curls through his fingers. Soft, so soft it felt and smelling of the herbs and spices she'd set

22

out for the cooks before she'd joined him on the battlements. Even as a young girl she'd carried those exotic scents on her skin. Even as a lad, he'd ached for her taste, for that unique perfume that called to him.

His lips caressing her neck, he removed the rest of her hairpins then massaged her scalp.

"Ahh." Turning her head, she nipped his forearm then laved the spot with her tongue. His cock twitched and she wiggled again. "I wish you would hurry."

"I'm making up for the first time we tupped. When all I could think about was shoving into you and spewing my cum deep within your cunt."

The vulgar word made her quiver from her shoulders to her ass. "I wanted that as much as you did."

"Perhaps, but I could have prepared you better." He let his hands roam over her belly until he could cup her breasts and feel her nipples pebble against his palms. Her breath hitched and she shifted restlessly, bringing her breasts more fully into his hands.

He plucked her nipples and savored her soft moan. He'd always loved the way her body responded to his touch.

"Gaspar. If you do not touch me soon—"

"I am touching you, Aida." He slid his hands into her open bodice and filled his hands with her warm, full breasts. Tilting her head back, he claimed her lips then filled her mouth with his questing tongue.

"Do you remember the first time I made love to you? Not the first time we fucked, but the first time I loved you with my hands and lips, with my fingers and my tongue?"

"Yessss."

"Tell me what you remember."

"We...we were sitting under the willow down by the river, completely hidden by the weeping limbs. You were holding me like this. Then you inched my skirts up—yes, just like you're doing now—and you stroked me there, put your finger deep within my cunny-burrow.

"Oh God, Gaspar, you feel so good." She spread her legs and arched her hips to take his finger deeper.

"And then?"

Her breath rasping, her hips bucking, she cried out in rapture. "I c-came, like I'm c-coming now."

When her spasms lessened, he whispered, "What happened next?"

"Y-you undressed me, laid me down on the blanket and... Gaspar, I am no longer that young girl. My body is no longer firm, my skin no longer—"

"You glow, dearling. I love to look at you, watch your nipples pucker when I simply wet my lips and stare at them. You are still the loveliest woman I have ever seen."

He pushed away her clothing just as he had that long-ago day. He laid her down on the pillows then drew her hand from her mons, her arm from her breasts. He stared at her, wet his lips and watched her eyes glaze and her nipples pucker. A blush spread over her lush body and his cock pulsed.

"Gaspar," she murmured, a gasp of embarrassment and longing escaping her sweet lips.

"Then I told you how your scent drove me wild, how it made of you a feast for me to devour. I ate you, just like I'm going to eat you now."

Kissing his way down her body, he savored every tremor, every sigh. He parted her nether curls and laved her clit. She bucked and dug her fingers into his shoulders. Her soft sighs grew louder and she writhed until he plunged into her spasming quim. She cried out while her sweet cum flowed over his tongue.

"And then?" he said, blowing a cool breath over her clit.

"Th-then you slid your hard, pulsing quim-sticker into my cunny-burrow and—yes, like that. Fuck me, Gaspar. Yes…just…like…that!"

Obeying her, no longer able to withstand her siren's call, he pumped deeper and deeper still until he spewed his cum into her pulsing core.

Sometime later, Aida shifted in his arms. "I'm getting too old, Gaspar, for floor tupping. Not even the pillows under me and you over me can keep me warm."

Gaspar slid his cock out of her then helped her to her feet. "If you'd eat more—food that is—you'd put some padding on those bones. We'd both be more comfortable."

"And you would start chasing Elita and Doretta all over the castle."

"What? Give up this haven?" He draped robes around them both, sat in the chair nearest the fire then pulled Aida into his lap. "You've made a home out of Kerrie's brothel."

He glanced around, savoring the warmth of the tapestries Aida had taken from her nieces' towers, flowers from Willa, horses from Pippa. When he looked at the sword-swinging knight glaring down from horseback on a hapless foot-soldier, he shivered. It was the mildest tapestry Yvonne had in her tower. Since Aida had wanted something from each of her girls, Yvonne had chosen to give her that one. But even that horror could not detract from the comfort Aida had created.

Aida laughed. "You mean you didn't enjoy Kerrie's tapestries with all the satyrs and centaurs ravishing the vestal virgins? Having chains and padlocks hanging from the bedposts did not arouse you?"

Gaspar held her tighter and kissed her neck. "When I was younger and Kerrie would call me here to go over the accounts I imagined…"

"Tupping my sister?" Aida said, unable to keep a hint of jealousy from her voice.

"God, no! I'd imagine you waiting for me in her bed, now your bed—"

"Our bed."

"Our bed." He grinned. "I'd imagine you there and my cock would harden and—Kerrie would laugh and send me off to find you. After three or four such sessions, she decided we should meet in surroundings more conducive to discussing matters of business."

"Then you never—?"

"Never. I didn't want her and she… Well, for all her love of men and sex, she knew I loved you. She would not embarrass either of us when I failed to achieve an erection."

"But she wouldn't let us marry," Aida said softly.

"No, she wouldn't. Perhaps she realized she would die young and didn't want you distracted from tending to the princesses by children of our own. Perhaps she was jealous of us, of our love. Who knows?"

"Hmmm."

"Why did she wait so long to marry?" Waiting for her answer, he toyed with her auburn curls, only beginning to show silver strands.

"I don't know the real reason, but I suspect she waited to vex our mother, who also married late, *ad nauseum* into Marchon history. We Marchon women are notoriously stubborn."

"As I've reason to know." He nuzzled her neck. She sighed and sank into him, completely relaxed. "Aida, do you suppose Kerrie forbade us marriage because…because I haven't a drop of noble blood in me?"

Aida twisted in his arms so she could see into his eyes, those kind blue eyes that had won her heart over twenty years ago. She ran her fingers through his close-cropped iron gray hair and kissed him gently. "You are the noblest man either Kerrie or I ever knew. No, Gaspar, I don't think noble blood had anything to do with her decision.

"Besides, of her three husbands only Willa's father Brecc was of noble blood. Alexandre, Yvonne's father, was a merchant, a purveyor of cloth and jewels. And spices. And Cesare, Pippa's sire, had only two qualities to recommend him—he painted as if inspired by all the angels in heaven and his golden hair fell nearly to his waist. Kerrie could rhapsodize for hours about Cesare's hair."

"And sexual prowess," Gaspar said then kissed her gently and drew her head to his shoulder. After a moment he chuckled and said, "Alexandre, Brecc, Cesare. Do you suppose Kerrie was working her way through the alphabet?"

Aida poked his ribs with her elbow then laughed with him. "What was number four's name? Donatien? No, Doran. Mercy, Gaspar, you may be right! And not only the alphabet, but through all of Europe, Alexandre from France, Brecc from England, Cesare from Italy and Doran from Greece."

Sobering, Gaspar said, "Perhaps we should allow the princesses the same freedom to choose their husbands."

"We cannot. Kerrie's instructions aside, where would the princesses meet these potential husbands? They refuse to leave Marchonland. It seems our best choice, our only choice, is to hold the tournament."

They sighed.

"All right," Gaspar finally said. "We hold the tournament and the field narrows, in accordance with Kerrie's wishes, to two. Which princess doesn't get a suitor? And how do the other princesses choose between the remaining two competitors?"

"With our assistance, Willa and Pippa will choose. Yvonne— Well, Kerrie left very specific instructions for her oldest daughter."

"I don't even want to think about Yvonne. And do I really want to know about Willa and Pippa? What does 'with our assistance' mean?"

"'With our assistance' means that all Kerrie had to say about her younger children was the choices must be limited to two."

"And?"

"Kerrie didn't say which princess gets which suitor. It falls, therefore, to us to decide on Willa's and Pippa's behalf. So long as each believes she has a choice." She shrugged then straddled him, her pussy hot and seeping juices over his stirring cock.

"I love that you still want me, Aida, with all the passion of our youth."

"I shall always love you passionately, Gaspar. To our dying day." She took him into her body and kissed him deeply. "You must, however, promise me one thing."

Already caught in passion, unable to say a word, Gaspar could only nod.

"You mustn't ride me to death until the girls are settled."

* * * * *

A month later

Gaspar leaned back in his chair in Aida's solar and surveyed the young lord sitting across from him. Lord Vinn wore garb fitting his station, a simple yet brilliantly white shirt under a wool jerkin and breeches in light gray wool. His high black boots were polished and, like the rest of his clothing, were of the finest quality. Gaspar liked that Vinn hadn't dressed fancily, but well enough to show respect for the princess and her family.

Aida sat at Gaspar's side, her face impassive, her hands folded and relaxed in her lap. She had chosen a gown of dark gray silk, simple in line yet elegant enough to flatter the suitors' sense of their own worth without showy splendor.

"Do you understand the rules of this next phase of the competition, Lord Vinn?" Gaspar said.

"I believe so. If I can persuade Princess Willa to relinquish her virginity to me I may marry her."

"If you wish to marry her. Which I assume you do or you wouldn't have entered the tournament. But I sense something about this situation troubles you."

"May I speak frankly? Thank you," he said when Aida and Gaspar nodded. "If I understand completely, I must complete the seduction before we may marry."

"Correct."

"That seems dishonorable."

"How so?" Aida said. "'Tis what her mother, may she rest in peace, wanted for her."

"But suppose… After we… Suppose she does not wish to marry me."

"Do you doubt your ability to seduce her?" Gaspar said.

Aida interrupted before Vinn could answer. "Will you define for us what you consider 'seduction' to mean?"

Lord Vinn slumped in his chair and, for a moment, seemed lost in thought. At last he learned forward again. "Seduction, in its most inclusive definition, to me at least, means engaging all of the princess' senses. She must, I believe, come to like me as well as desire me physically."

Gaspar permitted himself a small smile.

Aida leaned forward, her gaze intent on Vinn's face. "Why did you enter the tournament, Lord Vinn? What would marriage to Willa mean to you?"

"Honestly?" Vinn dragged his fingers through his dark brown hair. "As you know, Eyrie's lands adjoin Marchonland. For years I've watched my lands going lifeless while those of Marchonland produce crop after crop, year after year. My people can barely feed themselves, let alone feed my knights and men-at-arms.

"Since Willa is known as the holder of her lands, I hoped to win her—her knowledge and her ability to restore my lands to prosperity."

"You could have waged war on us," Gaspar said.

"To what purpose? Without Willa's knowledge Marchonland would, in time, no longer support its own people."

"We would have helped you had you asked."

"For what it's worth, I learned a man—a duke—does not ask for help. He takes what he must or goes wanting. This tournament seemed the means to have what I need without having to beg."

"Asking and begging are very different things, Lord Vinn," Aida murmured.

"But in this instance winning will gain me everything."

"If you win," Gaspar said, earning a brief, wry grin from the duke.

"Aye. If."

"Do you accept the terms, my lord?"

"I must. I do."

"Then we shall arrange for Princess Willa to meet with you in a day or two. In the meantime, please accept our hospitality."

"I must contact my captains," Vinn began.

"Dehy will carry any messages you wish to send. Other than that, you may have no outside contact. Barring a life-or-death emergency, of course."

"Do you still accept the terms?"

Vinn sighed then met their gazes. "Yes."

"Good," Gaspar said and smiled.

"Dehy will take you to your rooms and provide you with writing materials."

"Thank you," Vinn said. Sketching a brief bow, he left.

Seeing Aida's pleased smile, Gaspar could not resist teasing her. "He is perfect. For Pippa."

"Pippa?" Aida squeaked. "Pippa would eat him for breakfast then spit him out. He's too polite, too obsequious for Pippa."

"As Willa is too polite, as well. They will bore each other to tears in no time. On the other hand, Pippa will tear away that polite veneer to reveal the true man beneath."

"If she doesn't kill him first! No, Gaspar, Lord Vinn is for Willa. He has the patience to woo her—mind and body."

"I can't dissuade you?"

"No."

"Good. We're agreed then."

Aida poked his chest then kissed him soundly. "Perhaps we should wait to decide until we've met Lord Banan. Pippa will be more difficult to please."

"If only to thwart her mother's wishes for as long as possible," Gaspar agreed, nodding to Portier to admit Lord Banan.

The lordling sauntered in and Aida's heart sank. She had hoped Pippa would fare as well as Willa in this ridiculous marriage game Kerrie had devised. But this, this sneering fop, was beyond the pale. He wore blood-red velvet, doublet sleeves and breeches slashed to reveal cloth of gold beneath. His shoes had pointed toes and were slashed as well and covered with embroidered golden battleaxes.

Knowing her eyes would betray her disparaging thoughts, Aida lowered her lashes and sat without acknowledging him.

Gaspar sent her a puzzled look but introduced her. "Her royal highness Princess Aida is Princess Willa's guardian and aunt. I am Gaspar de—"

"My consort," Aida said.

"Highness. My lord. I am Lord Banan, Duke of—"

"Do you understand the rules of this phase of the competition, Lord Banan?"

"Yes. When I claim Princess Willa's maidenhead I shall claim her as my wife."

"Don't you mean if you are given her maidenhead, Lord Banan?" Aida snapped, looking up and taking in his finery. If clothes truly made the man, Pippa might find nothing to fault. Lord Banan's attitude, unfortunately, left much to be desired, at least in Aida's mind.

"That was my meaning, yes. But I don't doubt my ability to convince the princess that I am the man for her." He spread his arms as if to say, "Look at me. I am every maiden's dream".

Aida wanted to slap him.

Even Gaspar sounded testy when he said, "What do you hope to gain if you are successful and marry the princess?"

Banan blinked as if puzzled by the question. "Gain? Frankly, I hadn't thought of gain for myself. I suppose I will gain a lovely queen on my arm at court. A beautiful mother who will give me strong, handsome sons." He glanced at Aida and hastily added, "And beautiful daughters."

Aida thought Banan would rather gain the dowries of his future daughters-in-law than pay them out for his future daughters. Should he suffer the indignity of having them.

"Court? What court?" Gaspar asked, his tone sharp.

"Why, Marchonland's court, of course. The princess does hold court, doesn't she? No matter. When we are wed, we shall hold court frequently. Tournaments and balls as well."

"To what purpose?"

"Purpose?" As if sensing he was on treacherous ground, Banan frowned. "'Tis a pleasant way to pass the time. Although I must confess I don't enjoy the tedium of hearing my tenants' complaints."

A silence fell and threatened to become unbearable.

Gaspar cleared his throat then said, "You understand rape is not allowed."

Looking affronted, Banan said, "I wouldn't force myself on any woman, sir. Were I armed—"

"But you aren't armed and won't be during your entire stay. Do you agree or will you beg off now?"

"I beg for nothing, sir. I agree to all your terms."

"So be it," Aida said, waving Banan away.

When her doors closed behind him, Aida swore then said, "I have never met such a thoroughly disagreeable person in my entire life."

Gaspar grunted. "At least Pippa can't fault his looks."

"If he sneers at her like he did at us, she'll toss him out her windows."

"So we know now that Pippa can teach him manners. What can she learn from him?"

"Forbearance," Aida huffed.

"Perhaps we should give him to Yvonne."

Aida laughed. "Yvonne would cut him into little bits before—"

"She threw him out her windows."

"'Twould be the perfect solution," Aida said, sighing when Gaspar began to rub her tense neck and shoulders.

"We have another problem. Vinn and Banan must both believe they are wooing Willa."

"So?"

"How will Pippa react when her suitors continually call her by her sister's name?"

"Tell Pippa she'll have to get used to it. After all, she risked her life in the tournament. Masquerading as Willa should be like an easy canter for her."

"Even my hair is grinding its teeth."

"Allow me to provide something else for you to grind on," Gaspar whispered in her ear.

"Is planting your quim-sticker in my garden all you can think about?"

"Of course it is. I'm a man, aren't I?"

He pulsed against her cheek. She turned her head and sucked his cock into her mouth. That was the only answer he needed.

* * * * *

Willa's Tower

"Willa. Princess," Aida insisted later in a gentle but firm tone, "you must choose. Lord Vinn or Lord Banan?"

"Some choice!" Willa complained, turning from the casement window, a look of disgust on her normally serene face. "The Conqueror or The Slayer."

"At least there are now only two left to choose from." Aida replaced her niece at the bedroom window and surveyed the two encampments that nearly surrounded Marchon Castle. A mere ninety meters separated them. "And each is handsome and seems in good health."

"Which is more than I can say about my sisters!" Willa said, slanting Aida a condemning glare. "Had you and Gaspar not interfered, Pippa and Yvonne would not have been hurt during the competition."

"You cannot lay the blame at our feet, Willa. Had you and your sisters not come up with that harebrained scheme in the first place, no one would have been hurt. True, I did not think anyone or anything could unseat Pippa. But Yvonne could have been killed! Strong she may be, but she is no match for a man's strength. A bruised wrist is nothing compared to having a severed hand.

"Now no more procrastination, Willa. Lord Vinn or Lord Banan?"

"A pox on them both! Why can't they both go away? Court some woman who wants to surrender her freedom?"

"Not to mention her virginity." Aida sighed, more than a little wistful. She remembered being wooed and seduced. Gaspar, fortunately, continued in the role he had begun so many years ago, both friend and lover. "If you do not choose quickly, they'll have no choice but to attack or lay siege. Your people will suffer."

"I know, Aida. I know." After a long moment restlessly pacing her room, she said, "What does it signify if a man is skillful at seduction? Does it mean he will stay the course? Be faithful? Not beat his wife?"

"Alas, Willa, I know nothing about men other than Gaspar. I suspect, however, that if a man takes his time and truly wants to bring pleasure to the woman, those qualities may bode well for a long-lasting, satisfying union. They have augured well for me."

"Pfft! It means he will do whatever is necessary to ensure his own pleasure between her legs."

"Willa!"

"After the first time, are we not all alike? The gray cat in the darkness?"

"You have eavesdropped on the maids yet again," Aida observed with a small laugh.

"Nay, on the stable boys."

"Not to belabor the point—"

"Which you have done this sen'night!"

"You must decide, Willa. Your mother, may she rest in peace, left the choice with you. Most women of your station—"

"Yes, yes, I know. They have no say in who they wed. I only wish Mama's terms were less sexual. Whichever man makes me eager—eager!—is the man I must marry."

"I know you think it grossly unfair that you must bear this burden," Aida said. Your mother, may she—"

"Yes, yes, rest in peace. But I wager she's down there, fornicating with the devil himself and laughing her head off!"

"Willa!" Aida halfheartedly protested, for she envisioned dead Queen Kerrie doing much as Willa described, albeit in Heaven. "Nonetheless, Princess, you must do what must be done. You are the holder of the land."

"And Yvonne is the defender of the castle. Why can't she be the one? She is the oldest. And what about Pippa? She's the adventurous one, always riding out, who knows where, dressing like a boy and—"

"Like a boy, which is exactly the point. Willa, only the loveliest, the most feminine of you, stands a chance of avoiding war."

"But we all look alike! Except for the color of our eyes and some slight differences in height and build. And what if the man most able to arouse me has already been defeated?" she asked, almost wailing.

"Over that you have no control," Aida reminded her. "Your mother decreed that whoever wins you must also be strong enough to hold you safe. Lord Banan and Lord Vinn have proven their strength. The choice between them is yours to make."

"Damn, damn, damn," the princess swore with increasing vehemence. She sighed then said, "There is no other course. Invite them both to sup with me tonight. Here in my chamber."

"And after?"

"Have mercy, Aida! I am barely resigned to this step, let alone what needs to follow."

"You must have a plan, Willa. Will you first test them one at a time? Or both together before you spend time alone with each?"

Willa groaned and covered her heated face with her hands.

"If you test one first you may not be able to decide."

"Decide what?" the girl mumbled.

"If your arousal is due to the ministrations of the first or is truly and solely attributable to the second."

"Mercy, mercy, mercy," Willa pleaded loudly.

"May I make a suggestion?"

"Can I stop you? Yes! Suggest on!"

"See them both tonight then let them decide who will see you tomorrow or the following day."

"That sounds reasonable. But how will they decide between themselves? Having come this far, Aida, I cannot risk they will beat each other senseless."

"A game of chance, perhaps? Draw straws?"

"Hmm. Straws, yes. How then do we keep them from bodily harm while each waits his turn? Oh me, that does sound vain, doesn't it? Trust me, Aida, I do not place that high a price on myself, but I do value my people and our lands."

"Our lands, Willa?"

"Ours. We would not, could not sustain ourselves without those who work so long and hard on our behalf. And but for an accident of birth, you might rule here." Surveying her aunt's composed face and compact figure, Willa amended, "At least I could not exist without you."

"Thank you."

Sensing further discussion would only embarrass her companion, Willa said as mildly as she could, "Please see to tonight's arrangements, then return to help me dress."

Alone, Willa returned to her windows and gazed out at the two camps surrounding her and those she held dear. Each lord's shelter was easily identifiable in the warm spring twilight. Lord Vinn's black standard with gold gryphons rampant flew above his black and gold tent. Lord Banan's blood-red battleaxe adorned a golden banner over his white awning.

Did each pennant reveal the character of its lord? she wondered. The first a mythical creature, half-eagle, half-lion, without humanity, the second a weapon of destruction. Better, perhaps, to consider the colors of their tents, which she found no less discomforting, unfortunately. Was black for the Lord of Darkness, white for the Lord of Light?

Rubbing her aching temples, Willa sought comfort on her bed but sprang up as if she had sat on a burning coal. Like it or not, she would spend at least one night in it. Without sleep, if she believed the maids upon whom she'd eavesdropped.

Sitting instead on a high-back leather chair, she awaited Aida's return. And prayed her suitors would both refuse her invitation. Rhymes of "sup" and "tup" circled in her mind without mercy until she fell into oblivion and slept.

Pippa's Tower

"There you are, Pippa. And ready for your bath."

"What need have I of a bath, Aida? I'm only riding out again after I eat something. Yvonne's coming with me so we can discover what those two louts are planning." With a pointed glare at her aunt, Pippa rubbed her aching head where the iron ring had bested her after all.

"I swear, Pippa, I am getting too old to scurry down one set of stairs and up another."

"Meaning?" Pippa asked, suspicion in her voice but concern on her face. "Sit down, Aida, before you suffer an apoplexy. Now what do you mean?"

"Tonight is the night, Pippa, for you to meet your suitors. You do remember that, when Willa fell ill, the honor fell to you." The princess groaned and continued to glare at her. "If you don't consent, I shall have to try to persuade Yvonne to carry out your duty. One more trip down your stairs and up hers. Not to mention the other poor servants having to lug the tub from here to there. After they've emptied it here, of course. Then down to the kitchens for hot water and—"

"Yvonne has her own tub, as you well know. Besides, as the oldest, this onerous honor should fall to her."

"Under ordinary circumstances, perhaps. But your mother, may she rest… Don't frown, Pippa, or you'll look old before your time. As guardian of the horse, your mother had great faith in you. She knew you would make the best choice to ensure your bloodline remains strong."

"As she did? Besides, Kerrie died before any of us knew what our role would be for Marchonland."

"Your mother made the best choices available to her at the time."

"Do you know what they say in the stables, Aida? They say my mother rode all three husbands to their deaths. They say she would have done the same to husband four had they not died together."

"They all died happy."

"If that is happy, I'd rather die without ever knowing it."

Aida nearly groaned her frustration. She stood and smoothed her skirts. "Very well, Pippa, I shall go to Yvonne. I suppose she can learn how to choose what stallion to put with which mares. If, of course, her husband lets her keep them."

"What? Have you heard talk of this...this heresy?"

"There are two armies out there, Pippa. If one lord can mount the most men, it will give him a great advantage over the other."

"My horses." Pippa looked like she might weep at the thought. "No! I shan't allow either of those dolts to mistreat my horses in such a fashion.

"You need not climb any more stairs tonight, dear Aunt. I shall do my duty to my bloodline and to those of my horses. But bring the lords to me in the morning. I want the light of day by which to judge them."

"My knees thank you, Princess."

"Pfft!" Pippa spat.

Smiling, laughing to herself, Aida left the room and girded herself for one more set of stairs.

Yvonne's Tower

Puffing from exertion, Aida entered Yvonne's rooms and found weapons strewn over every flat surface in her solar. The girl herself was in her bedchamber, fastening on chain mail over her padded chest. She donned gloves of the same material, obviously having learned that even the most skilled swordsman could be wounded, even if unintentionally.

"What do you think, Aida?" Yvonne asked, her green eyes alight with merriment. "Will my men-at-arms declare me their queen of fashion?" At her waist bits of lace showed under the chain mail.

"Pippa might, were she to see you tonight. Which she won't."

"What do you mean, she won't?"

"Tonight's the night, Yvonne. Since Willa is ill and Pippa has a horrible headache, it is up to you to honor Kerrie's, may she rest in peace, last wishes. Tonight you meet the suitors."

"You mean I cannot creep into their camps, slit their throats and creep out again? Covered in their blood?"

She looked disappointed, but Aida knew Yvonne would never take a life unless she, or someone she loved, was threatened directly.

"Leave the slitting of throats to someone better at creeping. Stay with your bow, for you are the best with it."

"Pfft!" Yvonne said, but began to remove her armor.

Aida smiled. Of all the sisters, Yvonne was the most like their mother Kerrie. Some might call Yvonne vain and frivolous, for she loved fine clothes, music and flirting. Especially flirting. Threaten her or hers, however, and she was formidable.

"Are you sure neither Willa nor Pippa will see these men? And are you sure you want me to meet them? Willa is the most comely of us and the sweetest. And Pippa can at least speak of more than enhancements in weaponry. God knows most men like to talk about horses, with all the innuendoes that subject provides. 'Mount', 'ride' and so on."

"I believe 'swords' and 'spears' provide equal entertainment," Aida observed wryly. "With an occasional 'hammer' thrown in to keep the conversation lively."

"You think so?" Yvonne asked, hope in her eyes. Then she laughed. "Tease!"

"I have a surprise for you." When Yvonne looked at her with gleeful anticipation, Aida could not help but smile back. Even as a child Yvonne had been greedy. "It seems the king has decided to participate in this marriage process and is sending his own representative."

"He can't!"

The girl's vehemence startled Aida. "He is the king. He can do whatever he wishes."

"Whenever he wishes. Without even competing in the events that narrowed the field to two. Two, Aida, and only two. And I haven't forgotten that none of this would be open to discussion had you and Gaspar not interfered. Pippa and I would have won the tournament."

Ignoring Yvonne's tirade, Aida said, "Before you refuse, consider this. Look out the window and tell me what you see."

"Tents. Men milling about. Nothing's changed since yesterday. We are still surrounded." Shrugging, Yvonne turned away from the window.

"Look again. Use those archer's eyes."

"Hellfire and damnation! Those who surround us are also surrounded."

"And what lies between the inner and outer armies, Yvonne?"

"Our fields, our crops, our people. Damn those men! Damn them all to perdition!"

The girl raced to her garderobe and pulled out garment after garment from chest after chest, heedless of delicate fabrics and trims. "Where is the green silk gown, Aida? Where—"

"Wear the red. That way, after you slit their throats, the blood won't show. Save the green for your hanging."

"I do so enjoy the way your mind works, Aunt. Except for the hanging part." Grinning, she removed the red gown from her chest and flung her chain mail across her bed.

"While you bathe, Princess, I'll see to your gown."

On her way out, Aida signaled the maids to clear Yvonne's armor from the bed and to take every knife, sword and axe from her solar.

No sense tempting fate.

Chapter Three
Yvonne's Tower

&

Yvonne looked around her solar and felt a sudden urge to redecorate. Remembering how as a child the war-themed tapestries had frightened her, she wondered now how her suitors might view her chamber. Well, unfortunately, there was no time to weave new tapestries. Even if she'd had the inclination, tapestries took years to construct. Perhaps, once this ridiculous marriage game was settled, she would ask Aida if there were other tapestries she could hang here until Willa could design new ones and oversee their weaving.

She couldn't do anything about her chamber, but she could do something about herself. Greeting the suitors in chain mail might dissuade them for a time, but some part of her, the part that came from her innately feminine mother, wanted them to see the womanly side of her.

Going to her chest, she opened it and, for a moment, simply stared at the contents. The white silk with cloth of gold lining she wore for May Day and the harvest ball. Too formal for a first meeting, no matter how much she liked it and the way it made her feel like a fairy tale princess. She carefully removed it and laid it on her bed.

The pale- and dark-green silk brought a smile to her lips. Remembering Aida's comment about wearing it to her hanging brought Yvonne's hand to her throat. The red brocade renewed her smile and caused her to search the seams for places to hide her dagger. But no, she had resigned herself to the inevitable. She would marry — happily, she hoped and only once.

The king would send his representative, Aunt Aida had said. Would he expect Yvonne to treat him differently? Would she even know which of the three men was from the king?

Should she flirt with them? Kerrie would have and Yvonne knew she was enough like her mother to enjoy flirtation. She'd practiced on every man from Gaspar to the miller and knew, even when they knew her game, they enjoyed laughing with her.

But this situation was so different, Yvonne was at a loss. She gazed with longing at her chain mail but put it aside. Sighing, she took the green gown from the chest and went in search of Aida and her skills with ironing clothes and curling hair.

She wanted to make a good impression but—dear God—how much simpler life would be had she been born male.

Pippa's Tower

"Princess Willa?"

At the sound of Dehy's voice, Willa looked up from her embroidery and smiled sheepishly. She offered no explanation for being in Pippa's tower. In truth, she didn't know why Aida had sent her here with instructions not to leave.

"Princess Willa, I am Banan, Duke of—"

"Oh. I didn't expect to see you here, Lord Banan. I am not prepared to see you now." She looked down at her mud-stained hem then patted her hair and swept straggly tendrils behind her ears.

Not only did she feel dowdy, Lord Banan looked at her as if she were a frump without hope of ever looking any different than she did at this moment. Had he attended her last night, when she had expected him, he would have seen a very different woman, one who would have matched his fine dress instead of looking like she'd just returned from the fields. Which she had.

His obvious distaste made her doubt he could ever steel himself to court her, let alone seduce her. In truth, given his attitude, she doubted she could let him touch her. If she must carry through with her mother's ridiculous marriage scheme, she needed a man who could see beneath her clothes and— Oh dear, wasn't that precisely what he was doing? Trying to imagine her naked and still finding her lacking?

And the way his eyes kept shifting between her and Pippa's portrait of their mother put Willa off even more. None of her daughters could match their mother's beauty. It struck Willa as grossly unfair that Banan should judge her on two fronts at once and still not see her. Besides, he reminded her of Pippa's father Cesare, too blond, too pale for her taste.

"I apologize for interrupting you, Princess. Perhaps tomorrow?"

"Yes, tomorrow would be better. Please plan to break your fast with me tomorrow."

It seemed Lord Banan drew on every ounce of courtesy he could muster. He straightened to his formidable height then bowed over her hand. He could not, however, bring himself to kiss that hand. Willa, glancing down, saw that dirt rimmed her nails. Her first thought was that her new embroidery cloth must be stained with field mud.

"Until tomorrow," Lord Banan said, his haughty tone drawing her gaze to his face.

"Tomorrow, yes."

Dehy saw Lord Banan to the door then turned and winked at Willa. She covered her mouth until the door closed then gave way to laughter.

Willa's Tower

Pippa looked around Willa's solar and grinned. The room was so like her sister, warm and bright and welcoming. While Pippa seldom visited Willa's tower, she felt comfortable here, even alone and waiting for Willa to return from inspecting the wheat fields.

Pippa's smile widened when she saw the bouquet on Willa's table. Not touching the delicate dried petals, she sniffed and discovered the roses still retained a hint of their former, glorious scent. Yvonne had often described how their mother had looked when Willa's father Brecc presented this very bouquet to Kerrie on their wedding day. And how Willa had looked, years later, when Aida gave Kerrie's bouquet to her middle daughter.

A knock drew Pippa's gaze to the door. Puzzled that Willa would knock at her own door, Pippa called out for whoever it was to enter.

Dehy bowed in a tall man then closed the door, leaving Pippa alone with the stranger.

"Princess Willa?" he said in a low, frightening basso. He bowed over her hand and, straightening, smiled at her, apparently unfazed by her boy's clothing. "I am Vinn, Duke of—"

"Oh. Oh dear. I didn't expect you until tomorrow." She looked up at him in his gray wool finery then glanced down at her leather jerkin and breeches, at her muddy boots. Should she explain that she wasn't Willa, that she had just come from the stables to meet with her sister on some estate matter?

He frowned. She took a step back, suddenly intimidated by his size and dark handsomeness, by his intense gaze on her face. Oh dear God, how could she ever submit to this man when everything about him frightened her? He seemed a veritable giant and too dark a presence for her to feel comfortable.

"Please accept my apologies for this intrusion. I must have misunderstood."

"No apologies are needed, Lord Vinn," Pippa heard herself say as if from a great distance. She found herself standing at the door and holding it open. "Will you break your fast with me on the morrow?"

"As you wish, Princess Willa. Good night."

Dehy, standing outside the door, shot her a puzzled look then led the formidable Lord Vinn down the stairs.

Pippa closed the door then slid to the floor, feeling relieved to have escaped — at least for the moment.

Chapter Four
Pippa's Tower

&

"Where's the other one?" Pippa demanded, seeing Aida standing in the doorway to her bedchamber, only one man at her side. She smothered a sigh of relief that the dark stranger from last night was absent.

"Lord Vinn sent word, Princess Willa." The stress on "Willa" reminded Pippa that she must playact at being her sister. "One of his horses has fallen ill. He offers his apologies and begs you to indulge him tomorrow."

Suspicious of any statement that preyed on her love of horses, Pippa quirked one brow but turned her attention to the man. Her gaze ran over him. His short blond hair topped a rather pleasant face, his eyes the pale blue of late winter, his nose somewhat aggressive, his full lips curved into a smile that, in her estimation, bordered on a sneer. His white velvet doublet had slashed sleeves that bled red silk. She thought he must pad his shoulders, so wide did they seem. She avoided surveying his breeches and what might lie beneath them, but noticed that his silk hose were embroidered, his garters prettier than her own. Still, he did not intimidate her as Lord Vinn had last night.

"Then this popin—this poppet must be Lord Banan."

As the princess studied him, Banan glanced around her chamber. Judging by the tapestries, hangings he hadn't noticed in detail last night, she was exceedingly fond of horses. He did wonder, however, about the bit and bridle cast on the window seat. The bridle looked in need of repair but, surely, she did not intend to mend it herself. From the size of Marchonland's stables, visible through her windows, she must employ at least one saddler who could fix it.

Over the fireplace mantel hung the portrait he did remember. So the princess was not only haughty, she was so vain she must look at herself day and night. But there was something different about the portrait's eyes...

"Well, sir?" the princess snapped. "Have you nothing to say for yourself?"

"I would not refer to myself as either a popinjay or a poppet, Princess Willa. I am Banan, Duke of—"

"Yes, yes. These days everyone is a duke of this or that. I am amazed there are any lesser beings around to fight your battles. Is the meal ready, Aida? Then you may leave us."

"My lord. Princess."

Banan stood his ground, forcing this snooty female to brush against him in the doorway. Good thing he thought her beautiful or he'd not tolerate her bad manners. He found her boy's clothing appalling, but at least they and she were clean. So, thankfully, were her hands. But he would put up with almost anything for the pleasure of tupping her first. Which, thanks to Vinn's sick horse, Banan could do this very day.

Sick horse, pah! Most likely Vinn lacked the stomach to show himself the lesser man.

Banan held the princess's chair until she sat. Looking down at the generous curves of her breasts that showed through her worn but pressed cambric shirt, he considered caressing her, kissing those lovely mounds until she moaned with pleasure. Thinking her more likely to slap than moan, he settled across from her and gazed with admiration into her tawny eyes.

She frowned, obviously disapproving of his scrutiny, of his admiration which was only half-feigned. He quickly lowered his gaze to the laden trencher between them.

"Do you know Lord Vinn?"

Smothering his own frown, he said, "We have met at tournaments and the like. He lacks—"

"I do so admire a man who puts the needs of his horses above his own."

Schooling his face to seriousness, hoping it did not reveal his jealousy of Vinn, Banan said, "Alas, I cannot claim my horse's illness to gain your favor." The corners of her mouth twitched, making him cheer silently in celebration. At last he'd said something that won her approval.

"Before we begin, Lord Banan, we must discuss the rules."

"As you wish, Princess Wil—"

"The first rule being that you call me Pippa. Here, in these rooms, I wish us to be simply a man and a woman. Do you have a name you prefer over Banan?"

"I am not ashamed of my name," he began, but the flash of anger in her eyes stopped him. "I choose 'Aldo' to match your Italian 'Pippa'."

"That is very politic, 'Aldo'."

"I strive to please, 'Pippa'."

"We shall see, shan't we? That, after all, is the reason for our being here." She drew a deep breath then continued. "The second rule is not so much a rule as it is a concession on my part.

"I concede that, for the purpose of this exercise, you are the teacher and I the pupil. I will do whatever you ask of me, so long as it does not hurt me. You must agree that you will stop if I ask you to."

"I suggest that stopping may not be possible at certain points. I ask that you leave it to me to determine if you really mean stop."

"I always mean what I say, Aldo."

He raised an eyebrow at the challenge but said, "Very well. I agree, Pippa. Is that all?"

"I believe so." She chewed on her full lower lip then soothed it with the tip of her tongue.

He nearly groaned, the pain in his cock was that immediate, that sharp. He might die from arousal if preparing her took very long. The women of his experience never took overlong to convince, but he suspected this girl might test his patience and his control. But he was up for it—in more ways than one.

"Then we are agreed?" he asked.

"Yes." Her nervousness showed for the first time. She clasped her hands, her knuckles turning white.

"Perhaps we should begin by talking." He took her hand and led her to the well-padded window seat in her bedchamber. "What do you like to do, Pippa? How do you pass your days?"

"I like to ride whenever I can, much to Aida's dismay," she said, smiling up at him for the first time and motioning him to sit beside her. "If it is sunny as it has been this sen'night, my aunt slathers creams all over my skin to ensure my complexion is as pale as possible. She tries her best, but I shall never be as white as Wil—as is fashionable."

"I think your skin is a perfect color. It brings out the gold in your eyes. It is certainly soft," he added, letting his fingers linger on her cheek while she sipped wine from the cup he'd carried from her solar.

"And you, Lord—Aldo? How do you pass your days?"

"I train with my men. I ride, hunt, read."

"Read? You read?"

"I am, after all, your teacher."

"I meant no disrespect, Aldo. 'Tis only that most gentlemen of my acquaintance consider reading a waste of time."

"How then do these gentlemen manage their estates?" he asked angrily then quieted, soothed by her soft fingers on his lips.

"I suspect we will agree about the merits of reading, Aldo. But perhaps we should leave it for another time. I don't want to spoil our time together."

He kissed her fingertips then laughed. "I have an idea for our first lesson, Prin—Pippa. If you are willing."

Looking pale, she nodded. If what he suspected was true, her stomach was full of fluttering butterflies. Surprising him, so was his. He moved their table aside, placed several pillows against the wall of the window seat then leaned against them.

"Come sit on my lap." When she looked at him askance he said, "Will you break our agreement so soon, Pippa?

She still looked hesitant but complied, leaning against him when he pressed her head to his shoulder. The scent of lilacs drifted off her hair and skin. "Would you like me to read to you?"

It occurred to Pippa that she could read to him, but she decided to keep that fact to herself. He might deplore a lord not being able to read, he might not look so favorably upon a woman who could. Besides, his reading would allow her to discover whether he spoke the truth or merely bragged.

"I could send Dehy to look for something suitable."

"That won't be necessary for I have a small volume here." He made a harder job of drawing the book from beneath his doublet than was necessary. In the process he brushed his fingers over her breast, saw the nipple peak against the white cambric of her shirt, heard her soft gasp. His cock swelled, causing her to squirm and attempt to stand. He circled her waist with both arms and held her in place.

By the time he finished reading, he expected this prickly princess would be more than ready for piercing.

"Long, long ago," he began, noting how she leaned forward as if reading with him. He let her keep the illusion and cupped her left breast in his hand. So intent was she upon his book, she seemed unaware of his touch. But her hardening nipple against his palm told a more pleasing tale.

"I never saw so tiny a book," she said, raising tawny eyes filled with wonder to his face.

"One day I shall tell you its history." She laughed and wiggled her bottom against his cock. He swallowed his moan. Did she know what she did to him? No, she lacked that degree of sophistication. She was simply—and naturally—a hedonist.

"Long, long ago," she prompted.

"There was a beautiful princess whom every man desired. Isn't that what Willa means? Desired?"

Her prickly side resurfaced in the blink of an eye. "You broke the rules, Lord Banan!"

Pippa struggled to free herself but couldn't. Somehow, exactly how she couldn't say, she found herself under him and staring up at his blazing blue eyes. What she saw there was unlike anything she'd ever seen before in any man's eyes. Lust, she thought, breathless.

"I have changed my mind, Lord Banan. I wish to ride after all."

Ignoring her words, he kissed her with unexpected gentleness, so gentle a brushing of his lips over hers that she thought she'd only dreamed it. She gasped and his tongue swept into her mouth.

"Don't worry, Pippa. You will ride today, just not upon a horse."

The words shocked her. What shocked her even more was her reaction to the words. Her nipples tightened and anticipation swirled in her belly and moisture seeped — there, in what the stable boys called a cunt. His kiss made thought impossible and she surrendered without a fight or even a murmur of protest.

A pounding at her outer door made her shove Banan away.

"What?" she shouted, hurriedly smoothing her clothes and hair.

"The stallion, Princess. Your stallion has gone mad."

Marchon Pastures

Damn but the princess is fleet of foot, Banan thought, racing after her. Mayhap incidents like this stallion gone mad happened often and accounted, in part, for Pippa's choice of boys' clothing. Well, he'd soon take the horses and the princess in hand.

Gasping for breath, he watched her outdistance him and enjoyed the flexing of her firm buttocks under her worn, baggy breeches. There were some advantages to her outlandish garb, he admitted, strolling to her side in time to hear her order the chattering grooms and stable boys to silence. Some of them winced as if they'd bitten their tongues, but not one said another word.

He followed her gaze to the middle of the greening pasture. There, a coal-black stallion waged an all-out war on a dainty chestnut mare. The mare obviously wanted none of what the stallion offered. She kept sidling away, neighing and kicking and biting when the stallion came too near.

Banan took Pippa's arm and attempted to turn her away from the sight of the stallion's enormous erection. Like the mare, Pippa sidled away then strode toward the aroused male horse.

"Let her go," Gaspar ordered, appearing as if by magic and grabbing Banan's arm.

"That stallion will kill her!"

"No, he won't. He's used to her guiding him into the mare. And," Gaspar went on, holding Banan more firmly, "the mare is accustomed to doing Pippa's bidding. What Pippa needs now is quiet and time to decide if the mare is merely flirting or if she truly isn't ready. So shut up and stay still."

"Guiding him?" Banan muttered, appalled. But he quit struggling and tried to will away his own erection at the thought of Pippa guiding him into her welcoming warmth.

Pippa stood quietly, forming the tip of a triangle with the two horses. The horses had stopped, miraculously to Banan's mind, their "courtship" to stare at the princess.

"Pfft," Banan heard her say. To his complete amazement the stallion lowered his head, as contrite as a boy caught snitching cookies from the plate. The mare tossed her head, acting for all the world like Banan's sister flouncing away from a suitor.

"Pfft," she said again and made a shooing motion with her hands. The mare started toward Pippa who made another gesture that set both horses trotting away like children sent to the nursery without tea and cakes for comfort.

"Shall we catch them, Pippa?" Gaspar said, finally releasing Banan's arm.

"No. In a day or two they'll settle their differences and mate."

"In the field?" Banan's incredulity showed in his voice and on his face. "Those horses are too valuable—"

"'Tis not their first mating, Lord Banan," Pippa said coolly. "They'll come to the stables when they get hungry."

"But—"

"No matter what happens between us, Lord Banan, you'll have no say about my horses."

She considered him for a long moment. Her eyes darkened to a rich coffee color as if she found him lacking in every aspect. Had he not already learned she disliked flattery, he would have tried to charm her. Instead, he kept his expression blank and waited for her next salvo. He could be patient, he assured himself. But things would change once they had bedded and wedded.

"Look," she said at last, directing his attention to the horses.

The mare streaked across the meadow, her tail outstretched like a lady's ribbons in a wild breeze. The stallion ignored her until she wheeled around and charged at him, narrowly missing his hooves when he reared. She thundered by him, slowed to a trot, then stopped altogether. She looked at him as if to say, "Are you too tired now to do your duty?" then flicked her tail, inviting him to mount her.

Banan risked a glance at Pippa and saw a faint blush steal over her cheeks. Her nipples peaked against her shirt. Banan sighed in relief. This mating of her horses obviously had aroused his prickly princess, renewing Banan's hopes for a mating of his own.

"Perhaps we should allow them some privacy," he suggested, uncomfortably aware of his cock straining against his breeches.

"And obtain some for ourselves," Pippa murmured, her blush deepening.

Banan captured her hand and raised it to his lips. "In that regard, Pippa, we are in complete agreement."

Yvonne's Tower

"Well, this is a bit intimidating, isn't it?" Edgar said to his two companions. He ignored the scurrying footmen who carried food to the princess's inner chamber. "These tapestries are enough to give a man nightmares."

"No guts for blood, Edgar?" Gerard drawled, inspecting a different tapestry with a similar theme of men hacking each other to bits. He gave Edgar a contemptuous smile.

"And if the tapestries aren't enough," Gareth observed from the window, "you can watch your men training on the grounds below. If your eyes are sharp enough, you can see them bleed firsthand."

The men fell silent then shifted around the solar as if in a planned pattern.

"What do you suppose she does with these?" Gerard picked up several whetting stones then put them down and wiped his hands on a nearby cloth.

"The usual, I should imagine," Gareth said with a menacing grin. "Sharpens her knives, daggers, swords."

"Her fingernails, perhaps?" Edgar offered, falling in with the game.

"Now that has some possibilities," Gerard said.

They laughed and shifted again.

"Still, it seems an odd collection for a girl who fainted when that lad was unhorsed at the jousts," Gerard observed.

"Perhaps it's a holdover," Edgar said. "You know… Perhaps this was the old king's chamber."

"Marchonland has always been ruled by a woman," Gareth said, returning to the windows.

"Leave it to His Majesty—"

"Psst!" Gareth warned, hearing laughter in the outside hall. Not liking the unexpectedness or the direction from which the laughter came, he straightened. As did Gerard and Edgar. They all reached for swords they did not carry.

"My lords," a lovely creature said, her voice as melodious as a rippling stream, "I hope I've not kept you waiting o'erlong."

Slender grace, she seemed to float into the room.

How different she seems, Gareth thought. The girl at the jousts was like a ghost compared to this vibrant woman. Arrayed in a gown the color of new leaves that matched her eyes, her auburn tresses caught at her nape by a green velvet ribbon, she entered the room like a breath of spring—fresh and new, with a hint of summer heat on her face and ripe strawberries on her lips.

Edgar and Gerard looked as dumbstruck as Gareth felt.

She seemed struck speechless as well. Her gaze swept over Edgar and Gerard and her eyes widened as if she liked what she saw, a fact Gareth liked not at all.

Damn this ruse! This pretense that one of them was Vinn, the other Banan, the third a representative of the king. Gareth wanted her for himself! Damn it, she was meant for him.

What felt like an eternity later, she turned and looked at him. She blushed—blushed, by damn!—and lowered her splendid eyes to her feet. Did this maidenly demeanor bode well or ill for him?

"Aren't you all just the handsomest men in the world?" she said boldly as the three men bowed to her. All maidenly modesty had gone from her face. "What is your name, sweet one?"

"Edgar, luscious Willa."

Gareth groaned softly, the ruse exposed before the game began.

"A wealthy spear, eh? Are you aptly named, Edgar?" Lowering her gaze to his burgeoning breeches, she said, "Apparently so. Are you red-haired all over? We'll find out later," she said when he reached to undo his laces.

"And your name, tall, blond and endowed?"

"Gerard, beautiful Willa."

Now truly over. Damn them both for giving their real names.

"Another spear, eh? A hard one?"

"It gets harder," Gerard said.

She laughed and paced to Gareth. He said without prompting, "My name, glorious Willa, is Gareth and my spear is the strongest of all."

All her boldness fled. She looked up at him, her eyes confused. Now, surely, she would banish them all, exile them all. But, miracle of miracles, she drew a deep breath and smiled. Was it possible she didn't know the names of the winning competitors?

Idiot! She had fainted and been carried off before the dukes had revealed their names.

"Blowhard," muttered Edgar.

"Diehard," Gerard mumbled.

Gareth smirked.

"Gentlemen, please. There are only a few rules you must all obey. If any one of you breaks the rules, I will expel all of you from my chamber. Do you understand?"

Each nodded.

"Rule one, you must call me Yvonne. Rule two, you will be kind to one another. Who knows? Each of you may learn something of value from the others. Rule three, no violence — toward me or each other. Agreed?"

Edgar and Gerard glanced at solemn-faced Gareth then at each other. "Agreed," all three chorused.

"Good." She led them into her bedchamber and gestured at the table loaded with every delight imaginable. "We won't stand on ceremony, gentlemen. Serve yourselves."

"May we serve you first, Yvonne?" Gareth asked in a melodious baritone.

"If you wish."

There were several moments of elbowing. Edgar, being the shortest and slimmest of the three and therefore able to slip between the other two, emerged first.

"I thought we might share," his said, his voice sliding from tenor to baritone when she looked, first at what he had heaped upon the trencher then at his flushed face.

"Indeed, we might all share in Edgar's generosity," Yvonne said, gesturing for them to draw chairs around the small table Gerard brought from beside her bed. For a moment Gareth thought Gerard might make the table seem heavier than it was, but he set it down with a little grin and dragged up a chair.

Odd, Yvonne thought, they do not jostle for who sits next to me.

From her right, Edgar offered cheese and bread while from her left, Gerard held out a bite-sized piece of beef. Across from her Gareth sat, head bowed, both hands beneath the table. She soon discovered why.

In one hand he held her foot, while his other hand deftly removed her slipper, her garter and her stocking. He began to massage her foot.

"Mmmm," she sighed then started and looked at Edgar and Gerard in turn. Taking a bite from each of their offerings, she said, "Delicious."

Gareth looked up and winked. He reached out one hand for a chicken leg, but continued ministering to her arch. She closed her eyes and moaned.

While Gareth continued rubbing her foot and Gerard and Edgar kept feeding her, Yvonne studied them. Somehow she had expected them to dress more flamboyantly, to try to draw her attention by putting the others to shame. They hadn't. Each, it appeared, had garbed himself so as to be comfortable. Yet each wore clothing suitable for dining with a princess.

Edgar, who looked the youngest of the three, favored fine woolens in gold and brown, the autumn colors that enhanced his hair and eyes. Not surprising, Gerard had clothed himself in shades of blue velvet, slashed sleeves revealing cloth of gold, his cambric shirt finished at cuffs and collar with flowing, brilliantly white lace. His breeches were also puffed and slashed, his garters fancier than her own. The peacock of the three, but attractive nonetheless. He wore his clothing with careless elegance.

Careless elegance, she thought again, her gaze inexorably drawn to Gareth, dressed all in black, his only ornamentation a diamond-studded hoop in his left ear. Black, like the tent of one of the suitors surrounding the castle. If he was that suitor, which was the other? And who was from the king?

Gerard banged the table and shouted in a voice that surely hurt his throat. It assuredly hurt everyone's ears.

"Whatever you are doing, Gareth, stop it at once. He is cheating, Yvonne. Cheating!"

"I don't believe I said anything about not cheating," Yvonne said, smiling at each in turn.

Frowning, Edgar said, "Besides, if Gareth goes, so do we."

Gerard opened his mouth as if to argue further, then quickly closed it and learned back in his chair.

"I believe one of you brought a lute," Yvonne said into the lengthening silence. To her surprise Gerard raised a finger. "Wonderful. Unexpected, but wonderful. Do you sing, Gerard? Gareth? Edgar?"

Gerard and Gareth shook their heads, but Edgar nodded.

"Perhaps Gerard will play and Edgar will sing."

The two agreed with alacrity.

"What shall I do?" Gareth asked, sliding her slipper back on her foot.

Laughing, Yvonne kicked off both slippers and extended her feet. "You may continue cheating."

A pounding on her solar door halted them in the middle of a rousing song.

"It must be important," Yvonne said, "or they wouldn't disturb us."

She led the way to her outer door and found Dehy holding her chain mail and Aida carrying her bow and a quiver full of arrows.

"A company of twenty men is at the gate, Princess," Aida explained, striding into the room and motioning Dehy to follow her into Yvonne's bedchamber.

"What do they want?"

"They only demand admittance and will give no more information."

Yvonne paced after her people while Gareth, Gerard and Edgar tagged along. Her hands steady, although her heart beat rapidly at the potential threat to Marchonland, she loosened her laces and shed her gown.

"Tell them to go away," Edgar advised.

"Use you cannons to blast them to perdition," said Gerard.

Aida fastened the ties on Yvonne's padding then reached for the chain mail Gareth now held.

"I'll do it," he said, easily handling the heavy links and covering Yvonne's upper body. "Why all this hurry to fight, Princess?"

"I'm in no hurry to fight, Lord Gareth, and twenty men are no real threat. But those twenty, if allied with the four hundred surrounding us, could pose a danger. For your own safety, my lords, stay here."

"The devil we will!" Edgar shouted.

"Give us swords and we'll show them what's what," Gerard added, looking around for anything he could use as a weapon.

"What do you advise, Lord Gareth?"

"Invite them in," he said, his eyes darkening, his hand resting at his waist where sword and dagger would ordinarily reside.

"All at once?" Yvonne asked, liking the hint of danger that now surrounded him. Here was a man she could fight beside. No hothead like Gerard or eager pup like Edgar, but cool caution. "They will not come without their weapons," Yvonne said.

"Then we shall conduct our discourse from the battlements." Yvonne stiffened and Gareth added, "We shall remain in the background, of course, unless you need us. I suggest, however, that you position your men so that these intruders may be disarmed when they enter. If, that is, you cannot persuade them to enter already disarmed."

"Yes," Yvonne said, signaling Aida to advise Gaspar of the arrangements. "But what of the armies surrounding us?"

"I assume you have secret passages you can use to send messengers outside the castle. You needn't disclose them, Princess, merely send someone to the king's encampment. To Captain Cheney."

"With what message, my lord?"

Gareth, Yvonne noted, flicked a glance a Gerard, who held out his hand.

"Have your messenger give the captain this ring," Gerard said, opening his fist.

"Let me take it," Edgar said.

"No!" said Yvonne and Gareth together.

Yvonne added, "'Tis not that I distrust you, Edgar, but Marchonland's security demands the secret passages remain secret."

Looking abashed, Edgar nodded. "Of course, Princess. 'Tis only that I hate feeling useless. Stay here in your chambers—like a child. Stay hidden on the battlements—like a girl!"

Yvonne laughed.

"Your pardon, Princess. I meant no offense."

"None taken. My father used to rail at inactivity when Kerrie went into her defender mode. Since he was but a merchant, I can only imagine how a knight might feel."

"The ring, Princess," Gaspar said softly, magically appearing at her side. "Will you send it?"

"Of course. Are you certain no other message is required?"

Gerard and Edgar glanced at Gareth then all three nodded.

"Dehy," Yvonne called and the lad appeared. "You know what to do?" He nodded. "And to whom to give the ring? Then go."

The remaining five looked at each other for a long moment then Yvonne said, "Well, gentlemen, shall we see what our unexpected visitors want?"

They turned and made their way to the battlements. Her suitors stood out of sight. Yvonne advanced and looked over the wall at the armed men arrayed below her.

Gaspar strode to her side and called out, "State your business or you'll not gain admittance here."

A knight rode forward and unfurled the king's banner. "The king will not deal with a graybeard gigolo."

Yvonne swirled her tabard over her chest, revealing four golden towers against a field of green. Seizing her bow, she nocked an arrow and aimed at the knight. "Then deal with this, knave."

She loosed the arrow, planting it neatly between the fetlocks of the man's destrier. The horse reared then bolted before the knight could control it.

The remaining men, save one, backed their mounts out of arrow range. The one slid his hood back to reveal a crown of gleaming gold.

"I am the king," he said. "I have come to claim my bride."

* * * * *

Gaspar herded the suitors to Aida's tower while Aida accompanied her niece to hers.

Holding out her arms so Aida could slide the red silk bodice up her arms, Yvonne said, "Do you know anything about the king? Some fact only you and he would know?"

"No. Oh I know he was seven when you were born and your marriage was arranged. I know he has ruled Puttupon since his father's death five—no, six years ago. Like his father he is reputed to be a strong warrior and a great lover."

"Pfft! Am I to invite this intruder to kiss me to prove that he is or is not who he claims he is?"

"Why do you doubt him?"

"Ouch! Must you lace these stays so tight? As to doubt, Aida, I now doubt even you and Gaspar. Neither of you told me about an arranged marriage. One of the men attempting to seduce me is, according to you, the king's man. Yet here is the king himself claiming me as his bride.

"Doubt? How could I not doubt?"

Aida finished fastening a gold and diamond coronet to Yvonne's head. Sweeping her niece a deep curtsy, she then rose and said, "You'll think of something. You always do."

"Pfft! I want my dagger at my waist and make sure Gaspar has put my sword by the Princess Chair. Since we're allowing these armed men into the castle, I want my own arms at hand. And no more surprises!

"Oh do get up, Aida! You begin to resemble one of those bobbing birds Timms carves for his grandchildren."

With that Yvonne swept from the room, Aida on her heels.

Entering the great hall, Yvonne expelled her breath in a soft sigh, relieved to see her men arrayed strategically around the hall. The suitors, however, were nowhere in sight, leaving her feeling abandoned, although why she trusted them she didn't know.

Gaspar indicated her sword, which rested against the Princess Chair within easy reach. She sat. At her nod, footmen opened the wide twenty-foot-high double doors to admit the supposed king.

He entered with his phalanx of guards around him. They quickly stationed themselves so that each stood prepared to take on two of Yvonne's knights.

Her people bowed, but there was little if any respect shown. Yvonne, still seated, noted the man's scowl at her rudeness and mentally tallied a point in her favor. While he claimed his sovereignty, she knew her own. Here in Marchon Castle, at this moment, she sat in her mother's and sisters' place—queen of all of Marchonland and glad to be its defender.

"I am William," he announced to the hall. "King of Puttupon. Your liege lord and master."

He was short, this claimant to her body and her lands. And fat, even though he attempted to hide it under a loose tunic.

"I am Yvonne, Queen—"

"I know who you are. You are but a commoner, sired by a merchant and carried in a whore's womb. I shall make you my whore and teach you to fear me. Just as I taught her."

"Queen," Yvonne repeated as if William had not spoken, "of Marchonland." With a pointed nod to Gaspar she indicated the footmen should close the outer doors to the hall. She then continued, saying, "No man has ever ruled Marchonland. No man ever will rule here—especially not you."

A call to arms echoed through the hall. "To the king...the king...king."

Standing, seizing her sword, Yvonne called out, "To me, my friends. To me."

Men surged into the hall, charging through the doorways from each of the four towers that led to this room. Swords and halberks in hand, they quickly subdued William and his men.

"To the king," a captain shouted as Yvonne's suitors advanced from somewhere behind her.

"Pfft!" she swore, looking at them over her shoulder. "We need no assistance now."

Gareth took the sword from her suddenly limp grasp. "Of course not, my lady. We simply cannot resist the impulse to save a woman in distress."

She sank into the chair and drew deep, gulping breaths. Pfft! she thought, looking up into three smug male smiles, she still hadn't learned which of her suitors might be the king's man.

"Do you know this person?" She pointed at the quaking figure lying prone at her feet.

"Aye," her suitors chorused.

Yvonne blew out an impatient breath. "Who—"

"Your Majesty, if I may?" A weary-looking man with a captain's insignia on his tabard stepped forward.

"Captain Cheney, I believe."

"Aye, Majesty. This cur is the bastard brother of the true King of Puttupon."

"How did he come to be here? How does he dare to impersonate his king?"

"I can speak—" the cur in question began.

"When spoken to," Cheney said, planting a dung-encrusted boot on William's neck. From the stench, the captain and his men had come through the stables. "He eluded his keepers and, believing the king to be—"

Three coughs interrupted him.

"—visiting his cousins, he—"

"Those cousins, I believe, are here at Marchon Castle. Gaspar?"

"They are here, Prin—Majesty. Both suffering still from injuries Your Majesty inflicted during the tournament."

"Then why is he here?" She stood and again pointed at the man on the floor. He still struggled to free himself from Cheney's boot.

"I came to fuck a whore before—"

Cheney's fist silenced him. "If someone will show me where the dungeons are, I'll throw this foulmouthed... I'll see he gets there."

"I'll show you where to toss him." Gaspar sketched a bow. "Majesty. M'lords."

Watching them leave, Yvonne sank into her chair once more.

"Princess," Edgar said, kneeling at her feet and taking her trembling hand.

"Yvonne." Gerard's voice soothed her for a moment, but the sense of having been violated returned in a rush.

She felt lightheaded. Her stomach churned and she couldn't decide if she would throw up or faint first.

"Majesty." The humor in Gareth's voice brought her gaze to his solemn face. His sparkling eyes told her more

71

about his mood than his expression did. "You were magnificent. A lesser woman would have dissolved in tears, but you stood your ground. Now would you like to have him beheaded or would you prefer to flog him?"

She had to laugh, Gareth looked so sincere. "Personally flog him?"

"Yes. I'm sure we could find a whip in that palace you call a stable. Or, if you would rather, we could use the anvil as a chopping block and be done with him once and for all. Would you like that, Majesty?"

Behind the laconic delivery Yvonne heard seriousness and a willingness to stand with her whatever she decided. At last she shook her head and said, "I think I'll let the king deal with the putrid pustule."

The men laughed then Gareth said, "But?"

"Were he a better man, I'd meet him on the field of honor and skewer him!"

"Ahh, there's our princess. Fierce and bloodthirsty."

"You've made her cry, Gareth," Edgar protested.

"No," Gerard corrected. "She's merely relieved to have this unpleasantness behind her. Aren't you, Yvonne? Yvonne?"

Gareth caught her before she slid off her chair. "Be glad she fainted. I don't think any of us is ready to explain why William wants to fuck her—beyond the obvious."

"A pox on him!" Edgar swore.

"That's the problem, isn't it?" Gerard said. "He's so pox-riddled even his brain is infested."

Lifting Yvonne into his arms, Gareth said, "Make sure he's well-guarded. And if he escapes again... When you find him, skewer him."

Willa's Tower

The next morning Vinn entered Princess Willa's solar and looked around. Tapestries dominated the walls, their predominant theme that of flowers. Through the open casement he could see his own encampment and, beyond it, fields of tender spring wheat. Several embroidery frames were scattered over the table, the only apparent sign that the princess was not always as serene as she had seemed during the tournament. Last night she had not seemed serene at all, she'd seemed terrified of him. He hoped today she would be less nervous.

He heard voices from the inner chamber, paced to the doorway, but remained out of sight. A bed, resting between two casement windows, dominated this room. Pots sat on the sills, filled with tender green sprouts of some kind or another. Other than the bed, a window seat provided the only place to sit comfortably.

Hearing the princess's voice, he remained hidden.

"Where is he?" Willa asked. "Where is he? Where is he?" She despised the petulance in her voice, hated the urge to kick something, or better still, someone's hind end. "I understand why he could not attend me last night, but where is he now?"

"Lord Vinn, Princess?" Aida asked, gray eyes lit with teasing laughter.

"Yes, his ass—Lord Vinn, yes. Where is he?"

"Here, Princess Willa," said the object of her frenzy— nay, of her concern—from the doorway between her solar and her bedroom. "Have I kept you waiting?" His dark eyes told her he'd delayed on purpose, but what that purpose might be she could not imagine. Unless, of course, rudeness ruled him, as it had ruled the blond man last night.

"I feared…worried that our meal would cool before you arrived. You are just in time to save Dehy a trip to the kitchens. Quick and agile is our Dehy, but given to gossip and therefore to delay."

She squashed her sigh of relief that the blond fop she'd met last night was not with Lord Vinn. And at least her clothes and hands were clean. Her hair fell neatly over her shoulders. No mud clung to her boots or to her hem, but then she hadn't been to the fields yet this morning.

"Then I am grateful for my timeliness, tardy though it is."

Willa laughed and motioned him to sit with her at the table in her solar. "Might I ask what—?"

"I could not come to you until I'd washed away the scent of horses and of dreams."

"Pleasant dreams, Lord Vinn?"

"Very pleasant, Princess Willa, for they were of you."

"Leave us," she said, dismissing Aida and Dehy with a wave of her hand that, happily, also cooled her heated face.

"May I sit beside you, Princess Wil—?"

"If I may call you Vinn, you may call me Willa."

"Willa and Vinn it shall be then," he said. A seemingly inadvertent brush of his fingers on hers as they both reached for the same piece of bread renewed the heat in her face and brought a tingle to her hand.

"Is this how it begins, my lord—Vinn, I mean?" Oh dear, she thought, feeling a blush creep over her chest and face. Never had she been so bold. Was her strange behavior because she found him so much more attractive than Lord Banan?

"If you desire it, Willa." With his lips almost touching her cheek, he expelled a gentle breath over her ear. When she laughed and raised her shoulder as if to throw him off his intent he said, "Does this displease you, Willa?"

"It tickles," she admitted, her turquoise eyes wide and full of shy wonder.

"Then let us begin with something less... Nay, rather more benign. For example, you left your hair unbound and that pleases me. When I saw you at the jousts, your bound hair seemed almost as dark as my own. But when you moved from the shadow of your awning and into the sunlight I thought it full of molten gold. At first your skin looked like cold alabaster. Now I see that your hair is—"

"Red." She wrinkled her nose.

"Auburn," he corrected. His fingers drifted softly along her jaw, then sifted through her hair. "Auburn silk. And your skin is the rich color of the sweetest cream."

"Pretty words, my—Vinn."

"True words, Willa." He took another piece of bread, slathered it with butter then held it to her lips. "Open your mouth, sweet Willa. Let me feed you."

Before she could fully part her lips, his covered them. A feathery brush, another only slightly longer. Another, longer still, until her lips parted to allow the firm yet gentle intrusion of his tongue.

Gasping, she pulled away.

"Did I hurt you?" he asked, shifting as if something below his waist discomfited him.

"Too fast. You go too fast, Vinn."

"Then we shall proceed at a more leisurely pace. Do you wish to ask Aida to summon your minstrel?" When she shook her head, he suggested, "Shall we ride then?"

Something in his voice, in his eyes, hinted at a meaning beyond her meager understanding of the word.

"Some other day, perhaps. Today I think I would like to walk in the gardens with you."

"If it pleases you, Willa, so be it."

"Oh look, L—Vinn," Willa said when they reached the gardens. "The hyacinths are in bloom."

"Forgive me, Willa, but I know not one blossom from another."

"They're just there, one bed over. The pale ones—the pinks and lavenders and whites—remind me of proper princesses having tea and crumpets under their shady porticoes with only proper people at their side."

"And these others? Those of red and purple and gold, which I assume are the same sort of flower?"

Willa risked a glance at his face. Contradicting his somber visage, his dark eyes danced with humor. Had he enjoyed her poor alliterations, she wondered, feeling a blush steal up her throat. "Oh they are the most improper princesses, the ones who don't give a fig for propriety but dance all night in their colorful gowns and laugh so prettily, yet with restraint. They are bolder than their pale sisters and might venture beyond the ballroom, might allow a handsome stranger to hold their hand and—

"You are! Holding my hand, I mean."

"Yes and a very fine hand it is. Not too soft, not too small. A very lovely hand, all in all. The most perfect hand for holding. But you were about to say more, weren't you?"

"Only that… I forgot."

"No, Willa, you did not forget. You are simply too shy to ask for what you—for what the dashing, daring, improper princess truly wants from her hand-holding stranger."

"Do you know what that is, Vinn? For I swear I—"

76

"You do know, Willa." Still holding her hand, he turned her to him and brought her body nearer to his. "You have only to ask for what you want, lovely Willa, winsome Willa. You shall have whatever is in my power to give you." Tucking his finger under her chin, he willed her to look at him. Turquoise eyes wide, cheeks flushed, lips parting, she said the words he needed to hear.

"Will you kiss me again, Vinn?"

Relief and desire swept through him as he drew her slender but generously curved body to his own, rock-hard and pulsing with need to have her closer still. Remembering she was new to the ways of a man, he gently kissed her forehead, her brow, her cheeks, her neck. Finding the shell of her delicate ear, he laved it with his tongue then took the lobe between his teeth.

She groaned, half disappointment, half surrender.

"Does that tickle, Willa?" he whispered.

"No. I...I like it," she confessed in a small voice, "but..."

"But what, Willa? Do you want me to kiss your lips?"

"Yes. Yes, please!"

It took every ounce of restraint he had not to tumble her to the ground, toss her skirts over her breasts and plunge into her sweet, hot pussy. He could feel her body tremble and knew that anticipation rode her. The scent of her increasing arousal promised pleasure and release from his cock's torment. But he also knew she was not yet prepared for that invasion, the joining that would bring them both to that wondrous little death.

Instead, he repeated his earlier patterns. A brush of his lips against hers, moist and petal soft. Another, lingering an infinitesimal moment longer. Her lips parting, her tongue — pale pink and tantalizing — darting out, daring him, goading him. He growled, a feral sound that started in his chest and coursed up his throat. He claimed that wicked tongue, sucked it into his mouth, laved it with his own until her lips opened and she took him into her mouth.

She whimpered and he felt his control return like a bucket of water from an icy stream had been poured over his head. He held her away from his body, away from his pulsing cock that wanted to plunge into her.

"Are you hurt? Princess Willa, please forgive me," he said, drawing her back to him and pressing her head to his shoulder. He stroked his hands down her back, caught himself before his fingers could curl over her buttocks and learn those sweet, round contours.

"Forgive you for what, Vinn? I asked you to kiss me."

"Kiss you, yes. Not ravish you!"

"Did you ravish me, Lord Vinn?"

Vaguely unsettled by her question, he sought words that might erase the sudden sadness in her eyes. "Not exactly. I was, however, unconscionably rough with you. Your lips are swollen and red. And even though I shaved this morning, I've left whisker burns all over your lovely face."

"Will they fade, Vinn?" she asked, looking disappointed by the thought. "Does my face now displease you?"

"God, no! You look more beautiful than ever. And yes, the whisker burns will fade… Unless…"

"Unless?"

"Unless you wish to resume our kissing. I promise to be more gentle with you."

"Pfft!" she said then clamped her hands over her mouth.

"Princess Willa, I believe you enjoyed being 'ravished'."

"I believe I do—did. Enjoy it, I mean. Except…"

He waited for the words, longer than he had ever waited for a woman to tell him what she wanted. At wits end he nearly claimed those luscious lips, that tantalizing tongue.

"Except that I wonder, Vinn, if kissing is all there is to these matters. The maids claim that there is more but… Drat my runaway tongue!" A lovely blush suffused her face. She tried to push from his arms.

"Your tongue is perfect. Would you let it run away with mine?"

"Gladly. I mean— There I go again, behaving like a highly improper princess, not even asking what you might like."

"What pleases you pleases me. Except…"

"Except?" she prompted.

"If you want to learn more about 'these matters' we should find a place more private, more intimate, to continue the lessons."

"Lessons?" she said, her voice and eyes eager. "Then there is more to learn?"

"Much, much more."

"And will you teach me what pleases you?"

"If you study very hard to learn what gives you pleasure, I shall endeavor to return the favor." If, God willing, I survive.

A firm nod settled the matter and they made their way back to the castle, their pace quicker than before.

Gaspar met them at the lower door to Willa's tower. "One of the dams has broken. The south fields are flooding."

"I must go," she said, her expression caught between regret and urgency.

"I'll come with you," Vinn said. He ignored Gaspar's frown that suggested Vinn would only be in the way. He could do something to help, even if only to throw rocks to seal the breach.

Marchonland – The South Fields

Willa shielded her eyes from the blinding sun and surveyed the situation. Her tenants were hard at work already and had slowed the deluge somewhat. She ran toward the break, Vinn and Gaspar at her heels.

"What happened?" Vinn shouted.

"Later," Gaspar answered, panting in his effort to catch up to Willa.

"Timms, send Johnny for the shepherds then get the rest of the men to start tearing down that wall. We can use the stones to fill in the bank."

Timms scowled at her and muttered something Vinn barely heard on his way to do Willa's bidding. But he did hear Willa's shout.

"No ale this winter if you don't obey me!"

That got the men moving. In a comical manner they pushed at each other in their haste to reach the wall. Vinn discovered a dam breach was similar to fighting a fire at Eyrie. He soon had the men organized into a stone-brigade. Some stretched out along the stone fence, others lined up to pass their burdens along toward the broken dam.

Sheep soon appeared. Baaing, sniffing the air and seeming to lick their lips, they scanned the length of the fence as if looking for an easy path to dinner. Several jumped over a low spot and began to snuffle and chew their way toward drier shoots.

Gaspar waded through mud and rising water. Waving his arms and bellowing like a bull, he discouraged the sheep from jumping. They found another low spot and Vinn and some children added their voices to the mayhem to keep the sheep from jumping the fence.

Barking dogs and yelling shepherds joined the fray. What felt like hours, but was only a few minutes later, the only nearby sounds were grunts as the men passed along the stones. Growing fainter, the sounds of sheep, dogs and shepherds moved away.

"Enough!" Willa shouted and a cheer went up.

Vinn turned and dropped the heavy stone, barely missing his toes. Willa stood at the base of the sealed break, her hands above her head, her hair flowing like red-gold flames over her shoulders, her smiled wide and surrounded by caked mud. Her snapping fingers played a melody echoed by her swaying hips and dancing feet—a melody he thought only she could hear.

But apparently her men could hear it as well. They took up the rhythm and passed it up the slope to Vinn and his brigade. Even Gaspar caught it and clapped his hands in time with Willa's fingers and feet.

Vinn's breath caught in his throat and it felt like his heart was trying to thump its way out of his chest. This woman... This glorious woman played like a child who found joy in everything around her. Everything about her called out to him. She could ease his cares with a smile, take away every pain with a touch. He chuckled to himself. "Kiss it and make it better" took on a new meaning were Willa doing the kissing.

Damn him if he couldn't love her as well as want her.

Vinn heard another cheer and saw that the men had lifted Willa onto their shoulders and were carrying her up the slope. She smiled down at him then laughed when Timms and another man tumbled her into Vinn's arms.

"We'll need to rebuild the fence," Gaspar growled, looking like a year's effort was on offer.

"'Twill keep until tomorrow," Willa said, wiping at Vinn's face and leaving it even muddier. "The sheep— Put me down, Vinn. Please.

"The sheep are on their way to the summer meadows and the men have worked up a thirst. Gaspar, please see they are given as much," catching Gaspar's frown, she quickly said, "as their wives would allow them."

The men groaned then Timms asked, "What about our winter's ale, Princess?"

Willa frowned and looked like she was taking stock of the damaged sprouts. "I'm not positive, but I believe we'll have sufficient ale to last through this winter and the next. Thanks to all of you."

"And to your friend there," Timms said and led another cheer, this one for Vinn.

"Well done, Vinn," Willa said and pecked his cheek.

Vinn felt a blush seep over his face but sketched a bow to the crowd. Taking Willa's hand, he started toward the castle.

"I've never heard of making ale with wheat," he said as they trudged from mud to dry land.

Willa laughed. "'Twas barley you saved, for which all of us on Marchon lands thank you. We'd be sore pressed to winter without ale to warm us on stormy nights."

"I can think of something better than— Never mind," he said when she looked up at him, admiration in her turquoise eyes. He was nobody's hero, least of all hers, but she made him feel like one. "You might want to mortar those rocks when you can. They won't wash away so easily."

She hmmmed then tugged on his hand, forcing him to stop.

"Are you hurt, Willa? Do you need me to carry you or should I summon help?"

"I'm fine, Vinn. Truly. I just… I don't know how to thank you."

"For what?" Vinn felt thirteen again, when he'd fallen in love with Gareth's sister. He wanted to scuff his boot in the dirt. He knew if he said another word he'd stutter.

"For your quick thinking in forming those lines, for working alongside the other men."

She lowered her splendid eyes to the ground and he swore he'd never before seen lashes so long and thick. "I only did what any other…what anyone would do."

"Still, you knew what to do." She raised tear-filled eyes to his face. "I didn't. We'd have lost the entire crop if you…" Swiping at her tears, she rose on tiptoes and aimed a kiss at his cheek.

He turned his head and kissed her lips. "What you're feeling now is natural, Willa. 'Tis what a warrior feels once the battle's won. Relief that it's over, joy that we survived, sorrow that the battle was necessary." He kissed her again then, wrapping an arm around her waist, guided her once more toward the castle.

When they reached the outer door to her tower he bowed over her hand and reluctantly prepared to take his leave.

She caught his hands and seemed to stare at his chin. He tipped her face up and gently kissed her lips. He tried to pull away but she held fast to his hands, her strength surprising him.

"We need to eat, Vinn. Will you...will you sup with me?"

"Gladly, Willa, once I have bathed."

Even in the shadows cast by her tower he could see her blush.

"Will you...? 'Twould spare the servants were we to bathe together," she whispered so softly he had to lean even closer to her. "Will you?"

Expelling his held breath, he nodded and held open the door.

Chapter Five
Willa's Tower

ഌ

Vinn barred the solar door, lifted a flushed and laughing Willa into his arms and carried her into her bedchamber. He resisted the urge, the raging need of his engorged cock, to toss her on the bed and take her. He had promised her lessons and lessons he would give her. Even if they killed him.

He settled her in the alcove window seat, then knelt and placed her right foot on his knee.

"What are you doing?" She tried to jerk her foot from his grasp but unintentionally aided him in removing her boot.

"Under ordinary circumstances, your maid would help you to disrobe. Since she seems to be unavailable at the moment, I'll act in her stead. Unless you wish to summon her?"

"N-no. Please…" A gasp of pleasure escaped her lips when he removed her left boot and began to rub her foot. "Please continue."

"With pleasure," he said through a low chuckle. Sitting beside her, he shucked his own boots. "My disrobing would be accomplished by my valet. But since he isn't here at all, I shall have to soldier through on my own."

"I could have helped you with your boots."

"Perhaps later you can help me with other things." She blushed, correctly reading his intent, even though he suspected she did not truly understand. Yet.

"Is this…this disrobing of each other done only under extraordinary circumstances?" Settling on her heels, she studied him.

Others might find his face too stark to call handsome, but she liked that he was not pretty. His forehead was high, his eyebrows black slashes above his dark, dark eyes. Those eyes, she imagined, could strike fear—nay, terror—in a lesser man. But for her they had shown kindness, humor, patience and…oh dear, desire. His cheekbones and chin seemed to have been chiseled by expert hands, hands that knew the soul of this man. Strong, upright, unyielding. His lips were full yet firm and so gentle when he kissed her, so demanding when she needed him, wanted him to ravish her.

His body was that of a warrior, his shoulders wide enough to bear an ox's yoke or a woman's head. His arms were strong enough to crush the very breath from her, yet when he held her she felt safe. And his hands!

"It happens frequently when a man and a woman find themselves together and wish to remain alone." He settled his arm around her waist and urged her nearer. "Now just where did we leave off? Oh yes, I remember. I was nibbling on your ear and you were moaning, begging me to—"

"I wasn't! Nor were you nibbling on my ear. You were ravishing me, leaving whisker burns on my cheeks and chin and…and…"

"And you were moaning, laving my tongue with yours."

"Do it again. Please."

Without further preamble he kissed her, plundered her open mouth. She surged closer, fastened her fingers in his hair, encouraged him in every way she could.

Gentling his kisses, he let his fingers drift down the slender column of her neck then lower still until he cupped the warm fullness of her breast.

"Do you like me touching you? Say yes so we can continue."

"Yes!"

"Let me touch your skin there. Let me see your breasts and touch them without any barriers between them and my hands. I promise you'll like it even more. Will you? Let me?"

"Oh yes. Please."

"Please what?" In short order he dealt with her laces and the fabrics that kept him from his goal.

"Touch me. Oh!" she gasped when his tongue laved first one nipple then the other.

"Your breasts are beautiful. And I can see how much you like me touching them. See how your nipples poke out, begging me to suckle?"

"Yes, I… Oh yes. More, more, more."

In his wildest, most erotic fantasies, he had never imagined a woman could be so responsive. He had to see her naked, spread her legs and taste her sweet, intoxicating juices. He needed to bury his cock in her pussy, feel her milk him, take her cries of release into his mouth and fuck her until she came again and again and again. But he knew he needed to bring her higher first. He pushed her breasts together and moved his tongue over each peak in succession. Damn, he needed to come, if not in her, then between her magnificent breasts.

"Vinn, please stop. Vinn, I can't breathe. I cannot even think."

He groaned and somehow pulled back from the sharp edge of insanity.

"What?" he snapped in a sorely tried voice, shaking his head to throw off the haze of lust. But he would not let her settle or deny her own needs. "You don't want me to stop, do you? Stop touching you, licking you, sucking you."

To press his advantage, he gently pinched one nipple. It puckered immediately, proving his point without either of them saying a word.

"Now is an excellent time for you to pleasure me." Her dazed blue eyes lifted to his face. "First, you need to remove my shirt. Second, you must allow me to remove the rest of your clothing. Third, and this is most important, my beautiful Willa."

Her breasts rose and fell as if missing his attentions. He answered their call and resumed his assault upon Willa's senses. To his delight she tugged his shirt free of his breeches and nearly smothered him when she tried to pull it over his head while he still suckled her.

"Whoa," he laughed.

"Pfft! I am the clumsiest, most stupid student in the world."

"On the contrary, I am most impressed with your acumen. You do, I hope, recall what comes next."

"In your eyes I may seem both clumsy and stupid, but I am not a complete dunce," she said with a delightful pout that tempted him to kiss her. Which he did, sighing into her mouth when her naked breasts met his bare chest. Taking advantage of her wholehearted participation in their kiss, he untied her skirt and petticoat.

"Vinn! Vinn, I am naked." She tried to escape him and to cover her breasts and mons. To no avail.

"Lessons One and Two perfectly completed," he said, tangling his fingers in her hair and holding her immobile until she looked at him. Desire simmered in the turquoise depths of her eyes and almost decimated his vow to control himself.

She shivered, prompting him to ease her closer to him and rub his hands along her arms and down her slender back. At last, he thought, learning the roundness of her ass. Two perfect half-moons filled his hands. Those hands pressed her even closer, more firmly against his swollen, eager cock.

"Lesson Three." He held her at arm's length and back walked her to her bed.

"The most important, I remember."

He kissed her deeply, waiting until he felt her legs give way. "Lesson Three, you must lie down upon the bed."

"But, Vinn, I am naked."

"Perfectly, beautifully, sublimely naked." He nudged her backward until she lay sprawled, legs parted, her position nearly perfect for his next move on her. Nearly, but not yet perfect. The floor was too firm, too cold for his next maneuver. Joining her on the wide bed, he drew her against him, determined not to rush her.

Willa sighed and snuggled closer. She sighed again, puzzled that he seemed content to simply kiss her lips, to caress her swollen breasts and puckered nipples. She enjoyed that too, but she wanted him to... She didn't know precisely what she wanted. His hands made her breasts ache and her skin feel hot. His tongue exploring her mouth curled her toes, but that secret place between her thighs wept with yearning.

He had told her he would give her anything she asked for, but she couldn't form words she did not know. Sighing into his open mouth, she summoned her courage and covered the hand on her breast with hers. As if he knew how much that simple act cost her, his fingers released their gentle hold and let her guide them where she would.

For the moment she was content to rub his calloused fingers and palm over her belly and along her thigh. But soon even those light yet firm caresses were not enough. She wanted to cry, so inept did she feel, so incapable of taking care of her own body, her own...

She swallowed a sob. He stopped caressing her. She sobbed aloud then felt his fingers guide hers between her thighs. Together they touched her nub then stroked lower. Gratitude turned her sob into a sigh of pleasure. His low laugh vibrated against her earlobe.

For a heartbeat she thought of boxing his ears, but the idea blew away when he eased a thick finger inside that secret place now slick with her own juices. She spread her thighs wider and felt his whole hand cupping her, stroking her while his finger slid deeper, withdrew, then returned and circled within her. Frantic, feeling like she might leap off a precipice and fall to her death, her inner muscles flexed, her hips rose and fell with the rhythm of his hand.

"Don't fight it, sweeting," Vinn murmured. "Just let it happen."

"I...I... Oh yes." Did she cry out, whimper, scream? "Vinn, Vinn, Vinn."

"Tell me, sweeting. Tell me how you feel."

"I'm coming apart. Were you not holding me, I... Oh it's happening again."

Indeed, she was coming again. Great waves of torment and delight tightening her sweet pussy on his fingers. His control snapped. Holding her hands above her head, he positioned his cock at her entrance and dove into her spasming heat.

She looked up at him, her turquoise eyes wide with hurt surprise and shimmering tears.

"Sweeting, I did not mean to hurt you. I lost con—"

Her fingers on his lips stopped his apology. "The pain is almost gone, Vinn. And I'm glad you lost control. For a while I thought you didn't want me, that you kissed me, touched me, only to gather your courage to...do this to me."

"To hurt you?"

Her soft laugh tightened her pussy around his cock and he almost spewed his cum.

"I told you the pain is gone. I do, however, have a question for you."

She inhaled so deeply her nipples grazed his chest. He groaned and wondered how long he could keep from pumping, pounding into her. Her pussy was tight around him, hot and wet, his restraint on the verge of extinction.

"Yes?" he said when it seemed she awaited his permission to ask her question.

"Can your...appendage do what your finger did?"

Since his brain, what he had left of it, was centered on that very appendage, it took him a minute to figure out what she meant. "You mean, can my friend move in and out and around?"

"Uh huh."

"I'm certain he can, given the right encouragement."

"Which is?"

"Your heels on my ass."

"That's all?"

"You need to hurry or you'll have to wait some time for my friend to recover."

"Oh!" Her heels quickly met his ass and he began to move as she'd said she wanted. In and out, around, over and over again until she shouted his name and he spewed his seed deep within her. He collapsed against her, too weak for the moment to move.

When he'd regained his breath, he rolled to his side with Willa still in his arms, his friend still buried in her. And, miracle of miracle, seeming ready for more of her.

Willa felt his friend twitch and, still impaled, sat up. "Did you lie, Vinn? You said your friend needs time to recover, yet it seems to me he has recovered in a nonce."

"'Tis a tribute to you, sweet Willa. It shows how much we—I—desire you."

She turned the loveliest shade of pink Vinn had ever seen. His friend agreed, twitched and lengthened. Her eyes wide, her blush suffused her entire body and her pert nipples rose to kissable peaks.

"Vinn?" Her voice trembled. "Should I lie down again?"

"Nay, you're perfect as you are. Have you ever ridden astride?" When she nodded, he felt his grin widen. "Good. Ride me, Willa. Take me through the paces that bring you the most pleasure."

Placing his hands on her hips, he guided her movements up and down at a slow walk. "How does that feel, Willa?"

"Lovely, but can we go a little faster?"

"'Tis your ride, sweeting. You set the pace."

"I think I would like to trot." As she bounced up and down his shaft, her breasts bounced too.

He leaned forward, capturing one breast in his hand, the other in his mouth. She moaned and spread her legs. Taking him deeper, she slowed to a canter.

"Yessss. I like this best. Your friend so deep, then shallow, then deeper still, rubbing my nub, filling me. Oh Vinn, suck my nipples. Harder. Harder."

The untutored little vixen would drive him mad, but Vinn strove to give her all the pleasure she could stand. In return she gave him the words he craved and the wordless language their bodies spoke.

"I need to gallop."

"Yessss," she agreed and took him to a frantic pace. Breathless, she panted then cried out, "Yes. Yes. *Yes!*"

Their release seemed to go on forever. Vinn thought if he never took another breath, he would die the happiest man on Earth. Especially if he could hold sweet, sweaty, trembling Willa in his arms through all eternity.

Sometime later, Willa asked, her voice sleepy, "What lesson was this, Vinn?"

Stroking damp hair away from her face, he kissed the tip of her nose. "I cannot say. I believe the student has outrun the teacher."

"Pfft," she said against his chest, sounding pleased and replete.

Sometime later, she awoke to Vinn stroking between her thighs with a damp cloth. "Perhaps we should wait until we are truly finished," she suggested, feeling naughty and bold.

Propping his head on his hand, Vinn continued his ministrations and watched her expressive face. Lying — nay, sprawling across her blue duvet, she looked a veritable siren. Auburn curls lay helter-skelter over the pillows and her skin looked like creamy silk. Between her spread legs, her nether curls looked darker, even silkier than those on her head. Drops of cum, his and hers, still dampened those sweet curls. As he caressed them, her thick eyelashes fluttered closed and she hummed. When he slid his finger inside, her eyes flew open, their turquoise depths telling him she wanted him.

"Here." He grabbed a pillow and placed it in the center of the wide bed. "Now sit on it, then lie all the way back."

Slanting him a puzzled look, she rolled onto her stomach and crawled toward the pillow. He almost seized her hips to draw her back and take her like a stallion takes a mare.

She sat but covered her breasts. "I feel the perfect fool."

He shifted then stretched out at her side. "You are very nearly perfect." He tugged on a thick strand of her silky hair, wound it around his hand until she lay back and turned in his arms.

"Is this correct, Vinn?"

"Mmm," he muttered, nuzzling her neck and caressing her nipples. "I love the way you smell."

"L-lavender."

"Do you bathe in it, Willa?" Breathless, she could only nod. "What does it taste like?"

"T-taste?"

"To continue your lessons, I require your complete cooperation. If you think you cannot give me that, I can help you."

"How?"

"Stay just as you are and I'll show you." Thinking he should have planned this phase better, he willed his hands to steady, tore the lacings from her corset and returned to the bed.

"What are you doing, Vinn?"

"Ensuring your modesty does not disrupt your next trip to heaven. Hold still, sweet Willa. I promise I shan't hurt you." He kissed her palms then quickly wrapped her wrists with the laces and tied her to the headboard.

"Vinn, you're frightening me. If you do not release me this instant, I swear I'll scream the castle down around your ears."

"And I swear when you do scream—and I promise you shall—you'll be begging me for more."

She stopped trying to squirm away from him. When his knees hit the bed, she drew a deep breath and opened her mouth.

Perfect, he thought and slid his tongue between her lips. When he released her, her breath came in soft gasps from lips red and ravished. And when he slid his fingers over her nipples, she moaned.

"We are nearing the central point of this lesson," he whispered while he nipped her nipples. "Open your legs, Willa. Spread them as wide as you can. I promise you won't regret what happens when you do."

As he thought she would, she pressed her thighs together and glared up at him. "You promised you would cooperate," he said, smiling and hoping that would charm her into opening her legs.

"I made no such promise. You, on the other hand, promised you would... Pfft!"

"Help you to cooperate, yes." Staring down at her, he shrugged. "Very well, I shall persuade you to do what I ask. And I'll make you yet another promise."

She arched a brow then closed her eyes.

"When we review your studies in the future, you'll lie wherever I ask you and I won't need to persuade you to open your legs," he whispered in her ear.

Willa squeezed her eyes closed even tighter. Determined he would not persuade her with his mind-stealing kisses and talented tongue, she clenched her teeth.

If she could free her hands, she would box his ears until they rang.

"You promised me you wouldn't hurt me." She hated the desperation in her voice, hated even more that all her struggles had done was bury her hips deeper into the pillow beneath her. And even more, she despised that she could not stop staring at his…appendage.

Gesturing at his engorged cock, he said, "You know my friend here will not harm you, sweeting. He has hurt you as much as he will ever hurt you again. I promise."

"I begin to doubt your promises, Lord Vinn."

He laughed and lay on his back. That…thing he called his friend did seem to shrink a little and it ceased waving about like a banner in a stiff wind.

Sighing, the knave—the braggart!—tucked his arms under his head and sighed again. Looking down, he said, "Don't worry, dear friend. When the time is right you'll rise again." Turning his head, he grinned at Willa and said, "I promise."

"Please," Willa groaned. "Kindly cease making promises. I no longer believe you. All you want—"

"You know, it is truly sad that you have lost your faith in me. Just when I decided I must, as a nobleman, fulfill every one of my promises."

"Pfft!" She gazed at the canopy over her bed and wished the maids had been less thorough in cleaning her chamber. She could find neither a single spider web nor a dot of dust.

"You cannot be comfortable trussed that way." He freed her from the headboard then unwrapped her wrists. Kissing each in turn, he laved the marks with his clever tongue. "You have the most delicate skin, Willa. I should be flogged for mistreating you so."

"Aye, you should," she agreed, rising to her knees and, grabbing the offending pillow, smacked his wide shoulders with all her might. He laughed and she swung again. He made no move to defend himself but let her pummel him until she tired and tossed the pillow away. Sitting on her heels, she took stock of him and found him pleasing in every aspect.

"May I touch you, Lord Vinn?"

As if he didn't trust his voice, he nodded. His gaze followed her fingers as she traced the muscles in his arms and took one hand in both of hers. His fingers were long and sinewy, his palm rough with calluses. She could not help wondering if those very calluses gave her so much pleasure when he touched her.

Drawing a breath for courage, she grasped his wrists and guided his hands to those aching, needful orbs. When his fingers closed gently over them she sighed and looked up at him.

His eyes were closed and a frown furrowed his brow. She thought touching her displeased him until she glanced down his magnificent chest to the apex of his powerful thighs. There, his friend rose up and saluted.

"Could we continue?" she asked, unable to do more than whisper.

His eyes popped open. For a moment she feared he would tumble her backward and take her roughly, yet so sweetly. His eyes were so fierce she wanted to run.

Then he laughed and gently thumbed her hardening nipples. Moisture and need pooled between her legs.

"Your wish is my command."

"Then kiss me, Vinn. Please."

"So polite," he muttered, tumbling her backward, kissing her, stroking her, twining their legs so that his friend pulsed against her belly.

"Do you know that your breasts are so sensitive I believe I could make you come just by stroking them?"

"Come?" she breathed, savoring his hands on her, his lips, his teeth and tongue.

"Our primary goal. But no, I want your next time on my tongue, your juices in my mouth." He kissed her lips and stroked her breasts.

She moaned and her hips surged against him. She wanted…something. She didn't know what exactly, but she hoped, feverishly prayed he would know. And would give it to her. Soon. Now!

He kissed his way down her body. It seemed the most natural thing in the world to let her legs fall open. To feel his tongue touch that little nub that sometimes, when she washed there, gave her a brief jolt of pleasure. But this… This was no fleeting moment and pleasure was too weak a word for what she felt. His fingers worked their magic on her nipples while his tongue slid over that nub then into her.

"You taste like nectar," he praised then buried his tongue even deeper inside her.

She felt her muscles clench like they did before her horse flew over the first obstacle. Then they shattered and she flew into ecstasy.

"Vinn," she whispered, then yelled his name. Her hips surged against his face and release and relief flowed through her. Her body felt like melted candle wax.

He laughed and began again. Nub then opening, then something more. Harder, longer, while he sucked her nub and his fingers kneaded her breasts. She knew what to expect now and gladly let it come.

At the very height of her flight she felt him withdraw from her. She moaned in disappointment. Then something else, even larger and harder, pierced her. There was renewed pain at first, but then he kissed her and the path to heaven opened up again. In her mouth his tongue duplicated the thrust and parry of his hips. She widened her legs and took him deeper.

"Well done, Willa. All your lessons perfectly mastered." Laughing, he rolled to his back, taking her with him. Sprawled over him, too limp to move, she nuzzled his neck and fell asleep.

Chapter Six
Pippa's Tower

৪১

By the time Banan closed the solar door behind them, Pippa had lost her desire for sex. Nor did she want Banan's company. Unfortunately, unless she told him her true identity she could not dismiss him.

What had wrought this change? she wondered, ignoring Banan, yet all too aware of him. In the cheval mirror standing in the corner of her solar, she regarded his reflection.

He leaned against her outer door, seeming to study his fingernails. He appeared relaxed, but the set of his shoulders told a different tale.

"For some reason I cannot discern, you are upset with me."

She had expected him to act as if everything between them was fine, that he recognized the change in her lifted him, minimally, in her estimation.

"Is there a reason I should be upset with you?" She knew why. She was furious at his trying to dictate to her about her horses.

She saw realization cross his face before he eased away from the door. An indifferent yet somehow charming smile curved his lips. "No reason I can discern."

"'Tis obvious, Lord Banan, you dislike having to repeat yourself. Perhaps, however, you so enjoy the sound of your own voice it matters not what you say."

"Is your opinion of me as low as that?"

"Lower." For some reason she did not wish to insult him further and armored herself with silence. She paced to her window, retrieved a pair of spurs from the sill then spun the rowels. Banan, she saw from the corner of her eye, wandered aimlessly.

"To whom does this lute belong?"

Turning, she found him holding the instrument like he might hold a babe — with caution and longing. So he was careful of another's property, a point in his favor. "My sister. She sometimes plays for me."

"Does this sister have a name?"

Did he want anyone but Pippa? "Aye. But if you think to seduce her, you'd best go armed. Yvonne would gut you, clean her dagger on your fine doublet then serenade you while you bled to death."

His laugh matched the rippling notes he strummed. Dumbfounded, Pippa sank into a chair. Wishing him ignorant of her surprise, she flung one leg over the chair arm and swung her foot. The music he continued to play amazed her almost as much as his laugh had.

"Your sister must visit you often. The lute is in perfect tune."

Not knowing what to say to that, she said nothing.

A moment later a pillow plopped at her feet. Banan and the lute followed. She ignored him and studied the spur she still held. The rowels needed cleaning. She knew Dehy would see to it, but he'd also want them sharpened. She'd kept the spurs hidden and would clean them herself when she cleaned this unwanted human from her rooms.

Glancing down, she saw Banan's gaze intent upon the strings as his fingers caressed them. Would he be as careful with her body as he was with the instrument in his arms? The last rays of sunlight bathed his hair a golden hue and suddenly she wanted to touch it, to sift it through her fingers and test its texture. Unwilling to give in to this unwelcome impulse, she clenched the spur.

"Damn!" she swore, glaring at the blood oozing from her mount of Venus over her palm.

"Don't suck the wound," Banan commanded, quickly rising then returning with a wet cloth.

"I am not an idiot! I know I could poison myself by sucking on it."

"Not an idiot? Then why aren't those spurs with your farrier?"

"Because he would sharpen the rowels further and the horses would bleed instead of me."

"Little fool. Horses have thick hides, you don't." He wiped the blood away then peered at the small prick at the base of her thumb. Returning the cloth to the wound, he applied a firm pressure.

"I can do that," she insisted, trying to wrest her hand from his.

"'Tis my penance for upsetting you."

"Are you apologizing?" Somehow that surprised her even more than his laugh.

"Why should I? As far as I know I did nothing."

"Of course not!" She jerked on her hand but stilled when he placed a gentle kiss in her palm. "You said not to suck the wound."

"I'm kissing it to make it better." Once more on the pillow at her feet, he looked up at her, his pale blue eyes far too innocent for her to believe him. He wanted something. "Is it better?"

She started to tell him she didn't need a nanny, but his moist tongue across her palm distracted her. Her breath caught in her throat. Her fingers tingled and her nipples rose. Her rough cambric shirt rubbed against them when she shifted restlessly. With her free hand, she touched his hair, thick and silky. Then it drifted of its own accord to his cheek and rubbed the soft stubble on his jaw.

Somehow he had moved her so his body rested between her legs, his head on her breast, his breath hot on the peaking nipple his tongue laved through her shirt. She grabbed his ears, thinking to pull him away. Instead, she pressed him closer and arched into his avid mouth.

"My shirt... Ahh," she sighed when he pushed it aside then fastened his clever lips on her nipple. His rough palm held her other breast, his agile fingers kneading, stroking, gently plucking her.

Feeling cool air over her belly, she murmured a protest then didn't care that she no longer wore her breeches. And she sighed with pleasure when he pulled her hips forward. She missed his mouth and hands on her breasts, but only for the time it took him to comb her nether curls apart and plunge his tongue into her cunt. His fingers returned to strum her nipples and his tongue stroked that third nipple between her legs.

Something wondrously painful clenched her body, made every muscle tighten. She sobbed in frustration, knowing something more lay just out of reach.

"Relax, Pippa. It will come. You will come."

He lapped and plunged, plunged and lapped. Her thighs spread and her hands grappled in his hair as she pressed his head to her. Her hips rose and fell, searching, searching. And then it happened. Her body shook, delicious waves of tension grasped and released her cunt and she screamed his name over and over. She rode his tongue until, at last, the waves faded into lingering memory.

Opening her eyes, she found him grinning up at her and seeming greatly pleased with himself.

"It seems, Lord Banan, you are somewhat useful."

Again that surprising, youthful, joyous laugh. Then he plunged his tongue into her and it all began again. This time while he laved her, he slid his finger inside her cunt.

She tried to retreat from the pain but couldn't move. And soon that invasion changed to sweet torment as he eased his finger in and out, shallow, deep and deeper still. On the verge of shattering, she mindlessly obeyed his command to wrap her legs around his waist, her arms around his neck. When he lifted her, her weight forced his finger deep and she pumped her hips until she could only cry out in gratitude and slump against him.

When she no longer felt his arm around her, his finger in her, she moaned at the loss of his touch and opened her eyes. Sweet saints in heaven, he was magnificent. Propping bed pillows behind her back, she watched him disrobe.

Her earlier denigrating assessment that he padded his shoulders proved false. His were even wider, sloping into a muscular chest covered with golden curls between his flat brown nipples. Biceps flexing, he unlaced his breeches, Pippa's gaze followed his hands inching from his narrow waist to his powerful thighs, then sliding upward to free his cock.

She gasped. Even only half-erect, his cock seemed as enormous as her stallion's. Just thinking about where he intended to put that engorging, waving, seemingly eager mass renewed that wondrous pain in her. Yes, she feared it, yet she wanted it buried in her, moving in and out as had his finger.

"Banan," she whispered and his gaze fastened on her face. His pale blue eyes darkened, his predator's smile revealed even white teeth that looked capable of tearing her apart. Stalking toward her, stroking himself, his gaze intent on her, he said, "So that's the way of it, is it?"

She didn't bother to deny it. They both knew what she wanted. His smile even more feral, he placed one knee on the bed. "Take off your shirt."

She did and had the satisfaction of seeing his gaze arrow to her turgid nipples. Taunting him, she stroked them and bit back a moan. But he heard it.

"Open your legs and touch yourself there. I want to watch you, my passionate Pippa. I want to see how much you want me in your eyes, on your nipples. Hear you moan and beg me to take you."

Banan half expected her to refuse, but she obeyed him and did him one better. Moistening her finger, she slid it slowly into her. And all the while she watched him watch her make herself more ready for him than they both knew she was already.

Her red-gold tresses flowed over her breasts while her nipples played hide-and-seek amongst the curls. Her skin was flushed, damp with her rising need as she caressed herself, her eyes heavy-lidded, hiding her desire. Her long, slender legs trembled and she shifted restlessly.

"Open your eyes, Pippa. Yes, so I can see in those golden orbs how much you want me."

"Banan."

"Beg me, Pippa. Tell me how much you want me to fuck you."

"I want you, Banan. Need you. Please."

"Please what, Pippa? Say it."

"Fuck me, Banan. Please. Shove your cock in my cunt and fuck me."

Lifting her hand, he sucked the finger she had pushed within her. Even secondhand, her juices tasted sweet. He eased between her spread legs and rubbed his cock over her clit then seated the head in her hot, juicy, quivering opening. Her tawny eyes darkened before her gaze drifted down her body to where their bodies met. He shoved an inch or so deeper and saw her brief grimace of pain. Then she raised her gaze to his and begged him again.

"I know it will hurt, Banan. I don't care. Just do it. Thrust it in me quickly, then fuck me like we might never fuck again."

Unable to restrain himself any longer, he thrust deep, smothering her cry of pain with his mouth. He waited until she relaxed her lower body and ran her hands over his shoulders, down his back to grip his buttocks.

"Sweet saints in heaven, even your ass has muscles."

He chuckled and felt her cunt milk his cock. "The better to fuck you with," he said, withdrawing then plunging to his balls. "Say it again, Pippa. I like hearing your prim little mouth say the vulgar word."

"Fuck me, Banan. Fuck me, fuck me, fuck me. Merciful heavens, it's happening again. Good. So good. Yes, faster. Harder. Oh yes, Banan, fuck me."

Even with her nails digging into his ass, he thought he might die of the sweetest agony he had ever known. Her cunt milked him until his cock exploded. And yet he knew he could go on. He did and felt her cum flood over his spewing cock until she milked him dry and her spasms ceased.

They bathed in a copper tub of tepid water, uncaring that their playful washing of each other led to Pippa's straddling him and riding them both to completion. They ate a simple repast of cold beef, cheese and bread then made their way to her wide, tumbled bed.

Lying with Pippa snuggled against him, Banan sifted a skein of curls through his fingers and used the ends to tickle her nipple. It rose and puckered, daring him to suckle.

"Mmmm," Pippa moaned, pressing his head to her breast. He opened his mouth and sucked the nub into it. Soon, without his touching her anywhere else, he felt her body tremble against him as she reached yet another climax.

Sweet saints in heaven, what a splendid mistress she would make! He could train her to fulfill his every desire, have her whenever and wherever he wanted her. It would take months, years, before he tired of her. Hell, he might never tire of her. Besides, having brought her to ecstasy time after time, how could he ever relinquish her to another? He could not, he would not. He'd follow the king's orders to bed her and wed her. The king, his knights, needed her horses and Banan—as much as he wished to deny it—wanted her.

Her tongue in his bellybutton banished his musings. His cock rose to kiss her parting lips and clever tongue. Fastening his fingers in her hair, he pulled her off him. "Who taught you how to do that?"

"You are hurting me, Lord Banan."

But he could see in her eyes that more than his hand hurt her. Easing his grip, he started to apologize but instead said, "How did you know to do that?"

"I didn't know. I only thought that your lips and tongue gave me pleasure. I thought, mayhap, my lips and tongue could return the favor."

"They can. You may continue."

"I no longer want to." She turned away, only to find herself lying belly-to-belly, his cock throbbing against her cheek, his tongue licking her cunt. He laved her nub then sucked on it as if instructing her how to give him equal pleasure.

On a moan, she opened her mouth and drew him in. Lapping the head, she tasted salt, smelled the musky scent that told her he too was aroused.

He spread her open, then licked and sucked like he could not eat his fill. She duplicated the sweet torment and felt his cock pulse, felt a salty flow upon her tongue. His hips bucked, so did hers. Together they climaxed, shouting incoherently.

Drawing her up to lie against him face-to-face, he pressed her head to his shoulder. "Pippa, my precocious Pippa, what am I to do with you?"

"Fuck me, Lord Banan?"

Chapter Seven
Yvonne's Tower

so

Yvonne awoke to sunshine on her face and music coming from her solar. Content, she rolled to her side and pressed a kiss to the warm male chest beneath her cheek.

"Good morning, Yvonne."

Oh yes, she knew that voice. Its dark, sympathetic timbre had soothed her through a night of hellish dreams and now awakened her with tenderness.

"Good morning, Gareth."

A chuckle rumbled up his chest and vibrated against her cheek. "How did you know 'twas I?"

She sat up and swept her hair off her face. "Your voice kept me from madness. Your scent gave me succor. Your arms held me safe. After all that, I think I would know you anywhere."

"Gerard and Edgar would have done the same."

"Perhaps." She looked from his face to his chest cloaked only in dark curls. "But they, being gentlemen, would not have disrobed."

His eyes darkened. For a moment she thought she'd angered him, that he would yell at her or even strike her.

"Aye, they'd have remained clothed and branded your lovely face with their trims and laces." He ran gentle fingers across her forehead then cupped her cheek. "And, were I less a gentleman, I'd have undressed you as well."

Turning her head, she kissed his palm.

"I neither want nor need your gratitude, Yvonne."

Anger shot through her and destroyed every other emotion. "Too bad, for you have it." She scooted off the bed and smoothed her wrinkled skirts and bodice. "What have they done with," she couldn't say his name, "the pretender?"

"The king ordered him hanged."

The indifference in Gareth's voice sent a shiver through her. "So," she said, striving to match his coldness, "the king is nearby."

"Aye."

That and nothing more, damn him. "Aye, what? Will he now claim me as his bride, an arrangement I knew nothing about? Or will he only fuck me as that...other wanted to do?"

"I believe the king is an honorable man."

"And?"

"I believe the king believes in free choice." Gareth slid off the bed and retrieved his shirt from the floor.

"Pfft! I am damned tired of trying to pry information from you. What does the king intend to do? Should I prepare for a wedding or a war?" she shouted.

"That, Princess Yvonne, is up to you," Gerard said. Lifting his lute, he added, "'Tis said music soothes the savage—I can never remember if it's beast or breast. Whatever. I suggest we continue with last night's plans."

"But… Last night was intended for… You know."

"Seduction," Gareth said softly, his gaze on her heated face.

Yvonne felt her heartbeat in her throat. She wasn't sure she wanted any of this. What had happened last night she'd had no control over. But what might happen here, today, lay completely in her hands. If, of course, she could believe Gareth about the king and his intentions.

"I would like to change my clothes."

"Would you like help?" Edgar said, grinning hopefully.

"No," four voices said together.

Yvonne and the three men turned in unison to see Aida standing in the doorway, her arms filled with white silk and cloth of gold. "You men go and refresh yourselves. I'll see to the princess."

"You let us help last night," Edgar complained, nonetheless giving way to Aida's advance.

Grinning, Gerard and Gareth followed Edgar out the door. There, Gareth turned back and looked at Yvonne.

"I'm sorry," he said and quietly closed the door behind him.

Aida laid the gown on Yvonne's bed then opened the door to her garderobe. "Your bath awaits, Yvonne."

"Thank you, Aida." Tears clogged her throat and stung her eyes, but she refused to let them master her. Last night she had fainted—fainted for the first time in her life! Today she'd allow no weakness to undermine her. As for the king... She'd think about him later.

"Burn that," she said, waving away the red gown and stepping into the copper tub filled with steaming water and scented with rose oil. Yes, those should help take away her sense of being filthy.

"Do you want me to wash your hair, your back? Rub your neck?"

"No, thank you. I'll manage. I always do."

"I'm sorry, Yvonne. For my thoughtless words, for what happened last night."

Her voice sounding like it came from a great distance, Yvonne said, "The king has ordered him hanged."

"The sentence has been carried out," Aida said, soaping her niece's back. "Gaspar witnessed it, to be sure the bas—to be sure he didn't escape justice again."

"Again?" Yvonne sat up so suddenly water sloshed over the edges of the tub. "What do you know about this? I cannot bear to think of him but I must know." She turned and gripped Aida's hands. "Tell me!"

"He and G—the king's father courted your mother. The king, the old king, accepted Kerrie's rejection, his bastard did not. He raped your mother and later blamed her for his years of whoring, for the pox that ate away any trace of humanity."

"I see, but I don't understand. Why me?"

"I don't know, but I suspect he wanted to infect you so you would infect the present king."

"A perfect if convoluted revenge," Yvonne murmured, leaning back in the tub and beginning to relax under her aunt's ministrations. "The tale does, however, tell a disheartening story about the old king. To sire a bastard then, apparently, not care about him is unconscionable."

"He was barely a man when— Well, men have needs."

"So do women, but we control them. Mostly," she added, remembering her mother's appetites.

"The king, the present king, reputedly tried to befriend his half-brother. For his efforts the bastard attempted to murder him. Poison, Yvonne. No scars to help you identify which suitor may or may not be the king. Or if he is within the castle at all."

"Oh he is here," Yvonne said as she stepped out of the tub and wrapped herself in the towel Aida held out for her. "I don't know what game he plays, but I'll out him."

"Before or after he seduces you?"

"At this point, Aunt, I don't care which. I'll know and he'll know I know. That's all that matters to me now. Help me dress, Aida. I've a king to catch."

* * * * *

Yvonne doubted she had ever been so delightfully entertained in her life. For a man whose hands appeared too clumsy for anything more delicate than a battleaxe, Gerard's playing was magical. And while Edgar's speaking voice varied in pitch, his singing voice was a rich baritone. As for Gareth, his hands, like Gerard's, were magical too. And if he ventured higher than her feet... She felt too relaxed to object.

"Enough," Edgar said sometime later.

Yvonne managed to open one eye and discovered Gareth's hands were on her knees and the other two men stood glaring down at him.

"Princess Yvonne," Gerard said, drawing her gaze to his handsome face. "We men must decide how to proceed from here."

"Yes, we must," Edgar agreed, scowling at the other two.

"Gentlemen, remember the rules. No violence."

Gareth rose and said, "We customarily lead, but we've also learned to follow and to work in tandem when necessary."

Each sketched a bow then retreated to her solar.

She expected shouting but heard only their low voices, the words indistinct, unintelligible. Nerves began to war in her belly, but she fought them down. She was Yvonne, the archer — in her family, the bravest. So everyone thought. Just now, her emotions rioted and she wanted desperately to bolt. An hour on her training field would settle her nerves. Or she could let Aida and Gaspar decide which man might please her the most.

But no. These three had captured her attention when first she saw them. All tall, well-formed. Each handsome in his own way, each talented in his own way.

Edgar had endearing freckles across his nose and his eyes were amber, much like Pippa's only kinder. Gerard, all golden hair and bright blue eyes, looked like some Germanic god come down to earth to play with her. And as for Gareth with his sable hair and ebony eyes...He made her want to take away his burdens and make him laugh.

In truth, they were all, each in his separate way, reflections of her. In many ways she knew she was capable of kindness, like Edgar. And her sunny moods were often as bright as Gerard's smiles when he played his lute. And like Gareth, she needed kindness and laughter to lead her from the dark places in which she sometimes dwelled.

Hearing their footsteps, she straightened in her chair and folded her icy hands in her lap. With some trepidation she gazed at her solar door.

They entered one by one, stark naked. Magnificent! Wide of shoulder, narrow of hip, strong of thigh and calf. Their spears began to stir and her breath caught. Oh yes, she had chosen well.

"Look your fill," Edgar said.

"For you shall not," Gerard warned.

"See us again," Gareth intoned.

Together, smiling, they said, "Until we have made you scream with pleasure."

Yvonne thought she might scream right now, for the very sight of them made her nipples harden and moisture pool between her legs.

"Close your eyes." They commanded and she obeyed.

"'Tis not that we distrust you, Yvonne," Gareth said from behind her.

"We have decided your experience with us," Edgar muttered, drawing some silky fabric up her arm and over her cheek.

"Will be heightened if you cannot see," Gerard whispered in her ear.

"Only feel." Their voices blended in glorious harmony.

They blindfolded her.

Their hands ran over her from her hair to her slippers. Aida had dressed Yvonne in her second best court gown and had put up her hair in intricate curls. It would take a skilled lady's maid hours to undo her without damaging fabric or scalp. Yvonne expected the men would tire of the game long before she joined them in nudity.

Three unique sighs floated around her. She sensed the men circling her as if trying to decide where to begin disrobing her.

"Hair," someone — it sounded like Edgar — said.

"No. Her hair is so long and thick, 'twould only further hide what fastenings we must discover." That definitely was Gareth. No one else sounded so certain of obedience.

"We could ask her," Gerard suggested, sounding hopeful of an easy solution. She shook her head, determined not to aid in her own seduction, yet wanting, needing it to begin.

"If she would lift her skirts, we could undress her from the inside out." Edgar again.

"I think not. I've experience with this sort of frippery and know one must start where the effort ended."

Gareth, she fumed, wagering he had, indeed, more than enough experience with women's clothing.

"There's always tearing." Gerard sounded vexed enough to do just that.

Feeling strong hands on her shoulders, fearing their intent to rip her clothing from her body, she stiffened.

"Where's the fun in that? 'Tis too much like rape when our purpose is mutual pleasure."

Those hands—Gareth's?—massaged her shoulders then lingered at the tiny lump where her collarbone met her shoulder. That was the last knot Aida had tied before she hid it under the lace trim on Yvonne's gown.

"Ahh. I believe I've discovered a place to start unwrapping this pretty package. But first…" He turned her into his arms and pressed her against his body.

Even through her clothing, she felt warm skin and hard muscles, the hardest of which pulsed against her belly. She felt an answering quiver deep within her, yearning and moisture seeped between her thighs. Gentle fingers tilted her chin a breath before velvety lips brushed hers.

"I claim the first kiss," Gareth murmured against her ear, then reclaimed her lips in a kiss that made her toes curl inside her satin slippers.

For the space of a single heartbeat, she remembered she was being watched. Then she forgot everything and gave herself over to his masterful lips and tongue. She ran her fingers over his where they held her chin, over his hand, up and around his forearm to his biceps. There, the muscles trembled and flexed, their power making her both fearful and excited. Her nipples pebbled against her bodice and she ached to feel them against his powerful, naked chest.

A discreet cough followed by another, louder and more emphatic, overcame the buzzing in her ears. Reluctant but compelled by a sense of fairness, she curled her fingers around his and eased them from her face. Inhaling deeply, she took his scent, sandalwood and something uniquely Gareth, into her nostrils.

He sighed, a shaky exhalation. She felt him step away.

"Bring a chair and a candle," he commanded. "I think this is but the first of many Gordian knots."

"Shall I bring Alexander's sword?" Edgar, yes Edgar, asked.

"I think something less deadly," someone else said. "Something more like nimble fingers."

"Which gives you, Gerard, unfair advantage," Edgar complained while a noise like cracking knuckles reached her ears.

"All that lute playing is good for something!"

"No. Whoever finds the knot must untie it on his own."

"Giving you, Gareth, more time to touch her, to make her want you and only you? I think not."

Hearing the growing frustration in their voices, feeling her own frustration over every inch of her skin, Yvonne said, "Gentlemen, please. No violence."

When they quieted, she obeyed the press of hands — not Gareth's — on her shoulders and sat. "I know how to untie the knots," she admitted, feeling a blush creep over her chest and up her neck. Could they see it and know how nervous and excited she felt? "I propose we continue thusly. Each of you in rotation may find one knot. When you have discovered three, I shall untie all three until all the knots in time are undone."

"And let them grope whilst they search?"

"Not in my lifetime."

"On the pretext of trying to find a knot?"

"I know where each knot lies and shall give you hints. No one shall grope me, but each of you may kiss me when you succeed."

"And kiss the spot uncovered when you untie the knot."

Although none of the knots lay anywhere near those erotic points the maids talked about so avidly, anticipation blew the blush to her cheeks. Mayhap she would discover in herself more unique arousal points.

"And—"

"Yes, Gareth, each of you may kiss that spot."

"You peeked!" Edgar accused.

"I did not. I've simply learned your voices." When they said nothing, she added, "Mayhap the blindfold is no longer necessary."

"'Tis," they said as one. Someone grabbed her rising hands, another kept her seated, the third loosened then retied the blindfold over her eyes.

Someone leaned over her shoulder and murmured his breath hot on her ear, "Deprived of one sense, the others sharpen. Pleasure sharpens."

She inhaled. Gerard, she surmised, taking in the aroma of oranges from his breath. "You smell sweet, Gerard," she whispered back, nuzzling his cheek while his hand sought and found the knot on her right shoulder.

"Ach—I am not sweet!"

"Aye, sweet, with the lightest of touches upon my palate, leaving me hungry for thy tart sugar."

"Ah, lady," he sighed as he sought and found her mouth. Strong arms lifted her from her chair then let her body slide across his nakedness. She stood against him, exploring his heavy musculature and marveling at her lack of fear of him.

Was this how Kerrie had felt when Brecc first wooed her? Had Yvonne's mother known this leaping pulse, this need so different yet equally compelling to that she'd shared with Alexandre?

"My turn," Edgar insisted at the very moment Yvonne parted her lips to welcome Gerard's tongue in her mouth.

His massive arm releasing her, Gerard swept his rival aside, she heard Edgar stumble. Gerard deepened the kiss and when he disengaged from it, Yvonne tightened her grip on his waist to balance herself. He took a step away.

"You'll not find any knot below my breasts," she warned, angling her face at the last place she'd heard Edgar's voice.

"Then, lady, you must lift your arms."

Biting her tongue to suppress her startled gasp, she did as he demanded.

Edgar's fingers inched along the underside of her left arm. He clearly expected to find a third knot on the same side of her body that Gareth had discovered the first. He did and she felt victorious laughter tremble along his arm to hers.

And when he kissed her, she tasted that same victory on his lips. Oh she knew he wanted her. His kiss did not lack passion, but she sensed he wanted her more like a treasure taken from his elder companions than for herself.

Too well she understood that heady intoxication. Willa and Pippa often had exposed it in their expressions, so Yvonne recognized it now. Mayhap that was how Edgar evoked her urge to cuddle him to her breast and tunnel her fingers through his unruly russet locks. She badly wanted to soothe his heart as well as quell his desire to grow up too fast.

"Have I, princess? Have I found it, Yvonne?"

"Aye, you have found the third knot, Edgar. Now you all must either close your eyes or turn your backs so none can see how I untie each knot. Since I cannot see you, I must trust in you, my lords, not to cheat me. Or each other," she amended sensing their renewed bristling.

"We have turned our backs, Yvonne," Gerard said, his tone sullen.

"And are staring at your tapestry of Greek wrestlers," Edgar clarified, his voice less triumphant, making her believe he truly saw the two figures striving to castrate each other with their bare hands.

"Gareth?" she queried when he said nothing.

"My back is also turned."

"But? What more do you require?" Was that impatient voice hers? Yes! She would die of old age before they even finished disrobing her. And by then, not even Edgar would want her!

"That the rules be changed. That the last knot untied is the last place kissed by the first knot's discoverer."

She processed this puzzling demand then, attempting to clarify its intent, said, "Then you will place your kiss where Edgar found his knot. Gerard will—"

"Kiss where I discovered the first knot."

"And I," Edgar interrupted grudgingly, "as usual, suck hind teat."

Something in the tense silence made Yvonne smother a giggle. Forcing solemnity into her voice, she said, "Edgar, once I have loosed the ties, you may kiss my right shoulder. Gerard may then kiss my left shoulder. Gareth may then…"

Why, she wondered, did her voice turn breathy? She felt unable to draw a breath sufficient to fill her lungs. The mere thought of Gareth's lips on her skin made her nipples harden and her breasts swell.

And they were right. Blind, her skin felt more sensitive, her hearing sharper, her sense of smell more acute. They had only briefly tested her taste buds, but she expected they too would be keener.

"We are in accord, lady," Gareth announced. "Loose your knots."

Her fingers clumsy, she obeyed. "I am—"

"Do not touch yourself, lady. What happens henceforth you must leave to us."

Again, she sensed them circling her. Every muscle in her body clenched and she almost screamed when a fleeting touch grazed her right shoulder and gentle fingers slid her bodice down. Warms lips and a hot tongue lapped her neck then settled on the spot where Aida's knot had rested against Yvonne's flesh.

When she no longer felt his touch, she sighed again and sought to calm her racing heart. Young as he seemed, she knew Edgar did not lack experience. His touch, his kiss told her she would enjoy him.

Drawing a deep breath, striving to relax, she waited for Gerard's touch. Just when she thought he'd quit the room, a breath of oranges fanned her cheek and warmed her ear. "Ahh."

"Did you think I had deserted you?"

She shook her head and felt his hot, moist breath along her neck. The hairs on her nape, over her entire body rose like welcoming arms seeking his embrace.

He nipped her earlobe then pressed his lips and tongue against her left shoulder. When he sucked the tender spot she felt her bodice slip down her arms and moaned at the little ache he left on her skin. He said nothing, but she felt his satisfaction. Had his sucking marked her in some way, branded her as his?

Absolute silence reigned. She turned her head from side to side, striving to hear a soft footfall, a drawn breath, anything. She heard nothing. Not even a flutter disturbed the utter stillness.

From an undetermined source a voice whispered, "Raise your arm, Yvonne."

Without thought or protest she obeyed. Everything within her quieted as if her whole body held its breath. Then, although she had felt nothing, her left sleeve fell away, leaving her entire arm exposed to Gareth's warm kisses and moist tongue. He began at her fingertips and caressed, licked, kissed his way up the inside of her arm until he reached the exact location of the third knot.

Ripping off her blindfold, she glared at the top of his dark head. He ignored her and continued his ministrations to her flesh. She leaned over him, fastened her fingers in his thick, silky ebony locks and yanked his head up. She hissed, "Cheater."

To her dismay, the epithet sounded more pleased than censorious and her body celebrated his insolence. Her arm felt heavy and lethargic, as if his kisses had sapped her control of it. Every pulse point on her body thrummed like war drums pounding an erratic beat. Never in her life had she felt so confused. Never in her life had she felt so in tune with her body and its needs.

Standing on shaking legs, she reached inside her bodice and fumbled for the single string that would free her from the prison of her clothes. Three hands stopped her.

"'Tis not," Gareth began.

"Part of," Gerard continued.

"Our bargain," Edgar finished. "You did promise—"

"You would leave—"

"Your seduction up to us."

Gareth's hand remained on hers. Impatience riding her, she met his gaze and felt his lust wash over her like an ocean wave beating a helpless, immoveable shore.

"Then do it! Seduce me! I am not unwilling. I need—"

"You don't know what you need," Gareth said, his calm voice belying the heat in his eyes. "I—we do. Surrender impatience to us and we will give you everything you want. More even than you think you need."

"I want—"

"To feel your naked breasts against our chests. To let us touch and kiss every inch of your naked skin. To let our tongues lick your naked flesh everywhere, in places you have never dreamed of being touched, licked, kissed. We know."

Just the words made her weak with need. Groaning, Yvonne sank into the chair and buried her heated face in her hands. Moments later, still bent over her knees, she said, "I am not a child."

"If we considered you a child, we would not be here." Gareth hunkered down then pulled her hands from her face. "Kiss me," he said, quiet command in his voice, in his darkening ebony eyes.

She wiped her clammy, trembling hands on her skirts then touched his chest. His chest hair, curly and silky, tickled her palms as she raised her hands to his face. Tentative, she licked her lips then pressed them to his. Those firm, sculpted lips softened, opened to her shy probing then sucked her tongue into his mouth.

As if that kiss released them from a spell, Gerard and Edgar joined in the melee. Seconds later she felt cool air rush over her naked body and savored their calloused hands as they removed the last barriers between their skins and hers. As they had discovered the intricacies of her gown, they solved the mysteries of her hair. It fell over her shoulders, over her nipples, down her back. She laughed softly. These men, obviously, had no need of maids!

Someone, she knew not who, retied the blindfold over her eyes. She moaned a protest against Gerard's lips then gasped when the men lifted her and flung her into the air.

She shrieked at the suddenness of flight and laughed when she landed on her bed. She felt the mattress ropes give three times as each man joined her on the massive bed.

"Shhh," someone whispered.

Yvonne held her breath and waited for someone, anyone, to move. Unnerved by the total silence, she reached out, her fingers clutching at empty air until, at last, she found warm, hard flesh.

Someone's hand seized hers and guided it over his hairless chest to a nest of curls at the base of a pulsing length of rigid flesh.

"Oh my, Edgar, you are indeed a wealthy spear."

Muffled laughter wafted over her cheek. Another hand grasped hers and closed her fingers around an even longer, harder, wetter protuberance.

"And Gerard, you possess a truly hard spear."

"How—?" he sputtered, laughing.

"Cats can see in the dark," she teased, keeping the secret of their unique scents to herself.

She felt a warm presence at her naked back then felt something hot and hard slide between her thighs.

"Gareth, is that you?"

A deep chuckle reverberated against her throat. "Nay, 'tis Captain Cheney come to serve the king's consort."

"Come to service, more like," Gerard groused good-naturedly.

"Come to come, most likely," Edgar added, his voice husky as he encouraged Yvonne to stroke his cock.

"Come?" Surrounded by hot, hard bodies left her breathless. Feeling Gerard and Edgar pump their cocks within her hands while Gareth slid his between her nether lips made her weak and wet. Her nipples hardened and her breasts ached.

"Don't fret, sweet lady. Before the night is over you'll understand everything about coming."

With that raspy promise, Gareth palmed her breasts and stroked her distended nipples. Hearing her ragged breathing, feeling her juices flow along the length of his cock, he said, "Suckle her breasts while I— Yes, Yvonne, come for me." He spread her legs and slid his thick middle finger into her hot, slick cunt, making sure he stroked her clit as he moved his finger in and out.

"What is it?" she moaned. "Oh God. God. God!"

Easing her head back, Gareth took her cries of release into his mouth and felt his and his companions' sperm shoot over his hand between her trembling thighs.

"Oh," she sighed.

"I believe," Gerard said, his voice reveal satisfaction, "we could have made her come just sucking her nipples."

"Have you ever been with a woman so responsive?" Edgar asked of no one in particular.

Gareth's growl silenced further speculation.

Yvonne stretched and eased the blindfold from her eyes. Yawning, she murmured, "That was lovely. Thank you so much."

"We aren't through yet," Gareth said. Jerking his chin at the pile of her discarded clothing, he added, "Find her laces then bind her hands to the headboard."

"Gareth? There's no need… Please don't tie me. You're frightening me," she whispered, inching toward the edge of the massive bed and planning to run.

An implacable grip circled her ankle.

"No one will hurt you," Edgar promised.

"We just don't want you," Gerard began then glared at Gareth.

"To hurt yourself trying to escape pleasure."

"Why would anyone run from pleasure?" she wondered, giving up the struggle to free her hands from Gerard's and Edgar's steely grasps.

"Sometimes pleasure is painful," Gareth explained, testing the strength of her bindings. He quirked a brow at his companions when he realized her restraints were her own stockings.

"Then why seek pleasure in the first place?"

"Because it's pleasurable."

A trio of male guffaws made her grind her teeth. "I feel like a Christmas goose."

"About to have your head leave your body?"

"Nay. Dead already, plucked and trussed."

Edgar rejoined her on the bed, crawling from her feet to her head and trailing his fingers along her body.

She giggled. "You tickle."

"Keep your hands to yourself," Gareth ordered, making both Yvonne and Edgar scowl.

"St. Christopher on a crutch!" she swore when Edgar laid the blindfold on her chest then eased under her back. "Not that again."

"Yes, that again." Gerard chuckled as he handed the offensive cloth to Edgar. His fingertips grazed her nipples. They puckered, his cock throbbed, she moaned.

"You too, Gerard. Keep your hands to yourself."

"Where's the fun in that?"

"Besides," Yvonne observed in a breathy voice, "apparently hands are not required."

She could feel Edgar's cock hardening against her back and felt an answering tremor along her spine. Gerard simply stared at her and his spear grew as well, to an enormous length more suited to Pippa's stallion than a human man. What in heaven's name might he do with that? she wondered, tensing with fear and something akin to excitement.

Gareth appeared and offered her a damp cloth. Puzzled, she stared at it but from the corner of her eyes she could see his cock. Rigid as a lance, it thickened and rose to pulse against his belly. She knew she would die if he pierced her with that weapon, but—oh!—what a lovely death it would be.

"For your hands, Yvonne. You have our cum on your hands and between your legs."

"I'll wipe her," Gerard offered, earning another scowl from Gareth. "Or not."

"I'll see to myself."

To her own ears she sounded both haughty and breathless. When the men continued to stare at her, she sighed and consigned modesty to Hades. 'Twould do no good to ask them to close their eyes or turn away, they'd already seen all of her. Besides, knowing just the sight of her held them enthralled gave her a sense of power she'd never felt before.

Wiping each finger on each hand, she watched their eyes follow every stroke. When she finished with her hands, she drew the cloth over each breast and lingered for a moment at each burgeoning nipple before slowly drawing the cloth down her stomach to the apex of her thighs.

"God, I'm going to come again," Edgar, his chin on her shoulder, his lips against her ear, wiggled his hips.

A low laugh of her own escaped her lips as she opened her legs and stroked the cloth over that nub of pleasure Gareth had stroked to bring her to bliss.

"Oh dear God," she murmured as her body tensed in preparation for release.

"Enough!"

Gareth grabbed the cloth then flung it away. Edgar resettled the blindfold over her eyes. Two bodies made the bed ropes creak. As they'd promised, their hands touched her everywhere then roamed to touch her in other secret places. Their lips and tongues followed the paths blazed by their fingers. Someone sucked her nipples while another kissed her lips, his tongue danced with hers. A third stroked, kissed, licked his way down her body and held her thighs apart. Merciful heavens, was he staring at her there?

A hot tongue followed a cool breath over her nub then lapped at her like a cat at a bowl of cream. It took eager little sips then long and lazy ones, as if sated and seeking only the cream at the bottom. Like she was the cream and the bowl. Her juices gushed.

She forgot how to breathe, didn't know who did what, cared only that this exquisite assault on her senses never end. And yet she needed it to end—now!

"Yes, yes, yes! Oh God!" she cried, her hips rising and falling against someone's face, her fingers digging into naked hairy thighs, her body shattering apart like a thousand shards of glass, then drifting back to Earth, goose down floating on a zephyr.

Self-satisfied hums vibrated against her ear, her breast, her inner thigh.

"I think we'll need the cloth again," Gerard muttered at her breast, making her aware of the cum pooling at her back, along her thigh, beneath her still quivering legs.

"Leave cleaning 'til we're done," Gareth advised, sounding both sleepy and energized. He licked her thigh and she felt the longing build in her again.

"Besides," Edgar said through a yawn, "I'll need these juices to ease my way into her tight little ass."

Gerard laughed. "Sometimes hind teat isn't so bad, eh?"

"W-what?" Yvonne stammered, only then realizing her hands were free. But a moment later they were bound again, this time in front of her as she was rolled from her back to her belly. Someone shoved a pillow under her stomach while someone else—Edgar, she supposed—spread the cheeks of her ass then kissed her there. That fearful excitement invaded her again and made her shake.

Suspecting she looked like one of Pippa's mares presenting herself to a stallion, Yvonne thought she would die from mortification.

"There's something to be said for callow youth," Gareth drawled.

"Aye, recovery's quicker, albeit only a little," Gerard agreed.

"I find your jealousy flattering, however, I wonder when you ancients might wish to continue. We can't expect Yvonne to hold this position forever. She's trembling."

Two large hands, one larger and more calloused than the other, caressed each buttock then slid down the backs of her thighs. She flinched and bit back a nervous giggle.

"Edgar seems satisfied with ass for his treat."

"For starters anyway," Edgar agreed, tickling her anus and chuckling when her muscles clenched involuntarily.

Hearing nothing more, Yvonne felt her tremors intensify. Not knowing what would happen next had her stomach churning and her knees quaking.

"My lords, I fear her desire fades."

"Then we must renew it."

They gently raised her to her knees and parted her legs. She listed, was steadied, then felt a fleeting brush of silky hair along each thigh.

"Sit upon my lips, sweet lady. I'll take you again to paradise."

"Oh dear God," she moaned. Gareth's warm breath, his husky promise brought desire flooding through her.

"I'll suckle you now, Yvonne," Gerard said and suited word to action. Around her engorged areola, he said, "And one day soon I'll make you come only touching you here."

Something hard and wet invaded her anus and she howled.

"I'm sorry I hurt you," Edgar whispered then licked a tear from her cheek.

"'Tis gone now," she managed to say.

"Good." His hands on her ass, he pumped into her and everything around her, inside her, liquefied.

"More!" she cried. Their moans mingled. Her spasms racked her body even as Edgar pulled her backward and his hands held her thighs open wider.

Gerard's probing tongue swept into her mouth. He soon replaced it with a salty-tasting, quivering cock.

When Gareth drove into her she could not even scream. The pain, the pleasure were too intense. Through the haze in her mind it felt as if they all exploded simultaneously. Three shouts rang out, the fourth, her own, a muffled sigh. Moisture, hot and sticky, seeped from her lips, her ass, her womb.

Still joined, they panted in unison until, breath recovered, they eased apart, curled together like a litter of well-fed kittens and slept.

* * * * *

When she opened her eyes the next day she found the men all grinning at her. Huffing with indignation, she tried to sit up. Every muscle in her body protested. Hellfire and damnation! Over the three days of the tournament she had lifted her lance, joined a melee with her mace, battled numerous opponents with her broadsword. One night with these men and she could barely move. Moaning, she sank back against her pillows, closed her eyes and sighed loudly.

"Bartholomew's balls! What stinks?"

"We do."

"All of us, including you, Yvonne."

"And the bedding, of course."

"Of course, the bedding." She glared at each in turn.

Though her mind seemed mired in mud, her eyes saw what they had not discerned before.

Those smiles of satisfaction were the same. Those heavy-lidded, almond-shaped eyes, though different in color, were the same.

"You are brothers!" she accused then burst out laughing.

They frowned then Gareth said, "Same father, different mothers."

She could only laugh harder. Sobering at last, she said, "Game over, gentlemen. Which of you is the king?"

Gareth eased up her body until his head rested on her breast. Gerard propped his head on his hand and looked innocent. Edgar slid away to sit at her feet and play with her toes.

"He is," Gerard and Gareth said together and pointed at each other.

Yvonne fixed a stern gaze on Edgar.

He shrugged. "Forgive me, Yvonne, but I know you consider me too young and hotheaded to be the king."

"Which might better serve the king's purpose," she said, eyeing his youthful warrior's body with new appreciation for Kerrie's tastes in a variety of men.

"Which of you is the king?" she repeated, scowling at them all.

They turned their thumbs to their own chests. Grinning, they chorused, "I am."

Chapter Eight
Willa's Tower
❧

Vinn strode into Willa's bedchamber but halted in mid-stride, struck by the very sight of her. She lay on the window seat, her hair streaming like molten gold over the pillows, her eyes closed. The fingers of her right hand rubbed her nipples, stroking through the sheer fabric of her nightrail. Her left hand lay between her parted thighs. She moaned, a frustrated sound, and flopped both hands to her sides.

Vinn's breath caught and he tiptoed across the room. When he reached her side, he pivoted her and slid to his knees between her legs. Spreading her nether lips, he tongued her clit and slid his finger into her.

"Sweet cunny-burrow," he muttered. "Precious jampot, come for me. Milk my finger. That's it. Let go, cunny. Yes."

She bucked against his hand and screamed his name until her voice faded. She sobbed, "Vinn," and catapulted into his arms.

"What's wrong, dearling? Are you feeling neglected?"

"N-no. I am become a wanton," she cried, burrowing her face into his chest. "Like my mother."

"Why do you think that? Because you sought to bring yourself pleasure?"

She nodded and sobbed harder. "I...I thought if I could... You know, do that to myself, I wouldn't—"

"Need me," he said, gently pulling away from her. Her rejection hurt.

"No! I only thought… If I could, then I wouldn't want you so desperately that you're all I can think about. I was lying here, remembering how you touch me. Remembering how you make me feel when you touch me. Wondering how I will feel when you… You know."

"Put my cunny-catcher inside your cunny-burrow again."

"The words sound sweet, Vinn, unlike what I've overheard. They make me…hot."

"That's good, Willa. The words are meant to arouse you. There are cruder words, but I want you to know the sweetest first."

"Will the crude words also arouse me?"

Laughing, Vinn stood then sat on the window seat and spooned her between his legs. "We'll save that for a later time. Right now, I'd like to teach you how to please yourself. Now, when I arrived, your rail was here." He slid the hem until it rested high on her belly. "And your right hand was fondling your nipples. Which might feel better were you to open your gown and touch your skin."

He untied her laces then placed her hand on her naked breast. "Better? Yes, I can see you like that. Rub them, Willa. Rub your nipples and see them pout."

She moaned. "I do like that."

"Put your left hand between your legs and touch your clit."

"It doesn't feel as good as when you touch me."

"Then let me show you. Put your hand over mine and let your fingers follow mine." He touched the tip of her clit and her hips jerked upward. "Circle the little spot where uncle doodle goes."

"Uncle doodle?" She laughed, but her fingers followed his. Together they slid deep into her.

"Now rub, Willa. Rub your nipples and your clit. Slide your finger in and out of your hot cunt. Feel your juices flow."

"Oh God, Vinn! Vinn, I'm...!"

"Don't think about it. Just let it happen. Come for me, Willa. Let me see your face." He shifted until he sat between her knees. Her face was clenched as if in torment. Her hips surged upward then retreated. "Fuck yourself, Willa. Fuck yourself."

"Oh, oh, oh! Yessss!"

When she withdrew her finger her juices made a popping sound. Her scent drifted to him, lavender and aroused woman.

"Hold your breasts together, Willa. Quickly." Vinn freed his cock then drove it between her breasts as if buried deep inside her. She gently squeezed his balls and his cum spewed over her chest. "Willa, Willa, Willa. You are the most perfect wanton."

Pippa's Tower

Finding Pippa sprawled over her window seat, one hand at her breast, the other between her legs, Banan smiled. "You have turned into the perfect who—wanton," he corrected, seeing her eyes flash anger.

"You are interrupting my self-discovery, Lord Aldo. Go away," she demanded when he sat and put his hands on her knees. "Don't look at me."

"I cannot go away. That virago you call aunt has decreed we must spend a week together, our only respite from these rooms the stables. The stables!"

"I'm sure she meant we could ride together. Horses, Aldo."

"As for looking at you, 'tis no hardship when you smile."

"There?" she asked, pulling her nightrail over her knees to hide her mons.

"No, here," he said, leaning forward and kissing her cheek. "You have dimples, like the woman in the portrait. She isn't you, is she?"

"My mother. Most people think the portrait is of me. You may be more discerning than I credited you, Aldo."

He shrugged. "The other night, when I saw the portrait only in candlelight, I thought it was of you. I thought you vain for hanging it here, in your bedchamber where you could look at yourself day or night. But if you were truly vain, you'd have put it where everyone could admire it."

"Very astute. Shall we go riding?"

"Not yet. I need to show you that I am not such a popinjay as you believe. But you don't like talking about that picture."

"Exceedingly astute. I see you will not give way to another topic. So what is different about me?"

"Her eyes are gray, like your lady aunt Aida's. Yours are the color of molasses."

"The only gift I have from my father. He painted that picture."

"She loved him very much. You can see it in her eyes. She is daring him to see beyond her beauty, beneath the obvious allure and sensuality. He did. His love for her shines in her face."

"Yes, he loved her and she loved him. She loved him so well, she fucked him to death." Pippa sprang from the window seat and ran to the door. She could run no farther, blocked by her own modesty. A princess did not rush about in her nightgown, no matter how distraught she might be.

"If you hate her so much, why do you keep the portrait?" Banan asked, putting his hands on Pippa's heaving shoulders. He felt an odd little twinge in his chest, a twinge that made him want to hold her while she cried. While he could not escape her tears, he could grant her the opportunity for a tiny piece of privacy. So he didn't turn her into his arms and let her weep all over his chest. Instead, he handed her a handkerchief and rubbed her shoulders.

"I k-keep the portrait because my father p-painted it. Because it reminds me of the kind of woman I never want to become."

"What kind of woman is that?"

Pippa rounded on him in full fury. "The kind who cannot live without men. The kind who must have constant sex to feel beautiful. The kind... Go away! You don't understand. You can't!"

"Probably not, but I do understand this much, Pippa. You want very much to be loved as she was loved by your father."

"Pfft!"

"What does that mean? Pfft?"

"It means I don't like you. It means I'm too furious to swear at you. It means I am altogether too much like my mother, because if you don't kiss me—right now!—I'll—"

"Better?" he said when he had done as she asked. Nay, demanded, which pleased him very much.

"Better," she sighed. "I still don't like you but...I don't like you less than I did before."

He laughed and she blinked as if surprised by the sound. "'Tis a step in the right direction. I think. Now I think we should continue your lesson of self-discovery." He carried her to the bed and lay beside her.

"I cannot do it if you're going to watch."

"Then pretend I'm not here. Close your eyes. Touch yourself—your nipples, your clit. Remember what you liked best when I touched you. Think of the new ways you might like to be touched. Show me those ways so that I can please you even more next time. Yes, like that. Let it come. Yes. Now look at me. Pretend I'm in you, my *bacamarte* deep in your *val cava*."

"I want you there," she panted. "I want your milk-giving gun in my cave. Banan, please."

"Come for me first. Let me see you give yourself pleasure."

"Damn it, Banan! Oh, oh God!"

At last she quieted and lay with her hands still on her body. Her eyes glazed, she looked up and him and said weakly, "Pfft."

"What does 'Pfft' mean now?"

"It means this time I get to watch you. When you have finished pleasuring yourself, you may fuck me."

"If I do as you demand, you'll have to wait for me to fuck you."

She considered the idea for an endless moment. Then she sighed and pulled her nightrail over her head. Spreading her legs, she said, "Then you may fuck me first."

He waited in silence, willing his pulsing cock not to betray his need.

"Please, Banan," she said sweetly. "Please fuck me senseless."

He did.

Marchon Castle Training Grounds

"We need to go home, Gareth," Edgar said, panting. He wiped his borrowed sword with an oily rag then handed both to a hovering squire.

"Aye, we do," Gerard agreed, handing off his mace and shield.

"But why? Yvonne seems satisfied to have us all in her bed."

"But only you between her legs." Envy laced Edgar's voice.

"She came for you first, fucked you first," Gerard said, looking and sounding aggrieved yet resigned.

"You—either of you, or both for that matter—could have replaced me at any time."

"What? And have you flay me within an inch of my life," Gerard said, laughing.

"Besides, you're the oldest, the one most needing an heir."

"An heir," Gareth muttered. Surprising him, he found the idea more than tolerable. "I never thought of that."

"I imagine not," his brothers said, slapping his shoulders and nearly felling him.

"Besides," Gerard observed, "'tis obvious where the lady's preferences lie. She looks at you with those limpid green eyes as if you are the most succulent morsel she will ever taste."

"And you look at her the same way."

Gareth felt heat steal over his bare chest and face. "She does taste good. You know she does. Like apples and wine, you said," he reminded them.

"Meade," Edgar shot back.

"Honey," said Gerard.

"And you were the first to taste her cum."

"We think you should be the last."

"If she'll have you," said Edgar, for a moment looking like he hoped she wouldn't.

"Besides, we each want a woman of our own."

"Aye, a woman we can tup without having to share."

"A woman who will welcome our seed and give us babes to dandle on our knees."

"I-I never realized you felt that way," Gareth stammered.

"Hell," they said together and slapped his shoulders again, "neither did we."

"W-what if she won't have me?"

Laughing, Edgar said, "She has had you."

"Tell her she has no choice," Gerard counseled.

"No!" Gareth and Edgar yelled.

"No, the choice must be hers," Gareth said in a reasonable voice.

"Let us clean ourselves and let the lady choose." Arms slung over each others' shoulders, they made their way back to the castle.

Yvonne's Tower

Yvonne sat in her window seat and gazed down at the men on the practice field below her. Gareth and Gerard were going at each other with swords and maces while Edgar feinted in and out. Just whose side Edgar was on she couldn't tell, but she didn't like this too-real simulation of war. Any one of them could be injured or killed. She realized, for the first time in her life, that her own skills might one day be tested in a fight to the death.

How had Kerrie done it? Built and trained her own army? Fed troops and tenants alike? Bred and trained the horses that would carry her men into battle? Men and horses that might not return, but would lie in unmarked graves far from the fields of Marchonland.

Where had Kerrie found the courage to marry again and again? Had she done so because she lusted for them? Or had she recognized no one woman could defend, hold, guard at the same time? Had her husbands helped?

Yvonne could not imagine how they could have helped. Alexandre seldom resided at Marchonland, his business took him far and wide. And Brecc had his own people and lands to manage. Only Cesare had remained a constant in Kerrie's daily life, but he had no obvious skills to ease her load.

But, oh, how he had made them laugh! Perhaps that was where his value lay, easing burdens with the gift of laughter.

Dear God, she missed them. Alexandre always came home with tales of exotic customs. He smelled of spices and his pockets were always stuffed with trinkets for his wife and daughter. Brecc always seemed preoccupied with affairs of state, but he'd taken the time to teach Yvonne how to read and cipher. Gifts she had passed on to Willa and Pippa. And Cesare, sweet, laughing Cesare.

Pfft! Yvonne thought, brushing away a tear. She even missed Kerrie. She could see her mother's rapt attention when Alexandre told his stories, allowing Kerrie to envision places and people she would never visit, an escape she otherwise would never have had. And Brecc, his hands punctuating some obscure detail of law and Kerrie absorbing every word. Kerrie sitting at Cesare's feet, Yvonne at her side, Willa on Yvonne's lap and Pippa at her mother's breast. All of them, even baby Pippa, laughing at some silly jest he'd made.

'Twas more than lust, Yvonne realized. Each man completed Kerrie in ways she could not complete herself. Accidents or conscious choice? Yvonne didn't know. What she did know was that she wanted that sense of completion for herself.

Could she find it in one man?

Her gaze returned to the practice field and rested on a dark head. Was Gareth that man?

Propping pillows behind her back, she stretched out. Mercy, she was tired. She felt like she'd spent two weeks, day and night, on the training field. Which, in a way, she had.

No wonder Kerrie had stayed so slender, Yvonne thought. Sex was exercise, even if a great deal of it took place while lying down. It worked up a sweat and stretched muscles Yvonne hadn't realized she had. Just thinking of spreading her legs made her thighs quiver, but spread them she did.

A now familiar heat crept over her. Her breasts swelled and her nipples ached. Moisture seeped between her legs as if preparing for Gareth's penetration. If he were here now, who knew what she might do to him! She might not even give him time to disrobe. She might force him down on the bed, unlace his breeches and straddle him like she would her destrier.

Her hands seemed to take on their own life. They tugged at her skirt and petticoats until her hems rested above her belly. Then they loosened her bodice and touched her puckered nipples.

Oh God! She needed Gareth, wanted him in her, his cock easing in and out or plunging deeper and deeper until it seemed like she could feel him in her throat.

Gareth said, "I thought you'd be too sore to touch." He had come into her bedchamber and found her stroking herself.

"I am tender, but it still feels good. Only...I think it would feel even better if you touched me."

"Not this time. But, please, continue."

"While you watch? No. It's too embarrassing. You'll think..."

"What? That I might not always be around to pleasure you? That I'd prefer you take a lover than care for yourself?"

"I don't think I could. Take a lover, I mean."

"Then you'd better learn how to do it for yourself."

She sat up and rearranged her gown to cover her body. "Where are Edgar and Gerard?"

"On your practice field, trying to pummel each other into the ground."

"And you are here because?"

"I want to learn who you are, Yvonne. The woman who is eager to discover her sexuality?"

She considered him with a cool green gaze that reminded him of spring grass. "Yes, I am that woman." She chuckled and wrinkled her nose. "I never expected to be that woman, but I am."

"And are you also the woman who looks longingly down at Edgar and Gerard trying to kill each other?"

"I don't want them to kill each other."

"Then the longing is to be with them, pummeling and slashing."

She looked away then met his gaze head-on. "I am the defender of the cas—of the land."

"Who must slay dragons before she sleeps," he said, unable to squash the irony in his voice.

"In a manner of speaking." She sighed. Looking out the window, she said, "I am the protector."

"Of whom?"

Startled by the anger in his voice, she stared at him. "Of Marchonland. Of its people. Of—"

"Your sisters, Willa and Pippa? Are you the foolish woman who risked life and limb against Lord Vinn's sword? Against Lord Banan's battleaxe? Are you the idiot female who is lucky to have escaped with a few bruises? The same imbecile who wears this ring to cover the blow that could have severed her thumb?"

"I wear this ring because it was the first gift my father ever gave to my mother. It is the one thing she gave me that I truly cherish. As to the rest, yes. I am that foolish, idiotic imbecile who fought for her sisters."

"Why? Damn it, why?" He grabbed her shoulders, pulled her to her feet and shook her until she felt as if her teeth rattled.

"Because they belong here. Because what they do here matters. Each in her own way brings life to Marchonland, to our people. I am the bringer of death. Death is my duty."

"Pfft!" he said, making her laugh briefly. "Have you ever killed anyone? Fought a war? Destroyed a village? I thought not. Do you know why you have never had to do any of those things, Yvonne?"

"No. In truth, I never thought about it."

"Then it's time you do think about it. You've never had to do those things because…?"

"There's never been a need. Thank God."

"Thank yourself," he bellowed. "There's never been a need because you are prepared. Because you have trained

144

your men to keep Marchonland, your people, your sisters safe. No one has waged war on Marchonland because no one dares to fight you."

"How strange. How silly, really. How can you fear what you have never tested?"

"Exactly!"

"I thought I understood, but you've lost me."

"You! You're afraid of yourself. You're afraid of becoming your mother. But your mother was afraid too!"

"Maman, afraid? Ha!"

"Why do you think she married time after time? Or if she wasn't married, she always had a man in her bed. She was afraid of being alone."

"Next you'll tell me Maman was afraid of being alone because she never learned to pleasure herself."

I wasn't going to say that, but you may be right."

"You think I'm afraid of being alone."

"No, you're afraid of being with someone. With someone you care about, even love."

"I'm sure Maman loved Alexandre, my father. And Brecc and Cesare too. In fact, I'm sure, in her own way, she loved every man she ever took to her bed. But that—that lover of men, I am not."

"Nor shall you ever love one man. You're so afraid of becoming Kerrie, you fear being yourself."

"What does that mean? What do you want from me, Gareth?"

"I want you to be the woman I know you can be. I want you to leave Marchonland, knowing you leave it in hands as strong as your own. I want you to come with me, live with me. Willingly love me and only me.

"But you can't, can you? You'd rather die here, in Marchon Castle, on Marchon land, than risk living."

Yvonne rubbed her aching temples and sank onto the window seat. "But I thought... I thought this was about sex."

"In part it is about sex. But do you honestly believe you could give me your virginity without giving me at least a piece of your heart?"

"I didn't know it was you. I couldn't see. Remember? You and your brothers blindfolded me."

"You knew, Yvonne. Even truly blind, your body would know me. You're just too much a coward to admit it."

"I'm not a coward!"

"Prove it. Leave Marchonland and come with me."

"I-I want to but I can't. I love you. I truly do, but I can't leave Marchonland."

"Why not? See, you are a coward."

"Gareth, you don't understand."

"Then make me understand, Yvonne."

"Here, I have purpose. What purpose would I have in your country? To sit idly while you wage war for your king? To raise our children alone? To pray for you? To want you every second of every minute, of every hour, day, week, year?

"Damn it, I do love you! I do. But I haven't a talent for embroidery or tending crops as Willa does. And were it not for my destrier, I would hate all the horses Pippa loves so well, cares for so well. What would I do?"

Gareth paced away then returned to her side. Tucking his finger under her chin, he forced her to look at him.

"I thought you might train my—my king's men. With your fierce reputation to support me—I mean, to support my king, I'd never have to go to war. We can raise our children together. Be together every minute of every hour of every year."

She narrowed her eyes, looking every bit as fierce as the tales told of her. "You liar. Train my king's men, support my king. You blackguard, you are the king.

"Pfft! Pfft! Pfft!" she hissed.

"What is this 'Pfft'? All you Marchon women use it, but what does it mean?"

"It means whatever it needs to mean at the moment."

"Then what does it mean now?"

"It means I love you. I'll train your men, raise your children and defend you to my dying day."

"Thank God!"

"Thank yourself," she parroted. "But if you go back on your word to let me train your men, I'll make you suffer."

"Will you? How? Cut off my cock?"

"Worse. I'll fuck myself and make you watch."

Laughing, he swept her into his arms and carried her to the bed.

"Rest assured, my fierce archer, I'll not break my word to you. In the meantime, I think we need to clean up your language."

"You mean?"

"Fuck is something we do together. It's like making love. Together."

"Hmmm. Then what do you call it when I'm alone and need to… You know."

"Unnecessary."

Chapter Nine

ഌ

Willa stooped to examine a blade of what Vinn assumed was wheat. Today she wore homespun wool the dull shade of dung and sturdy boots. He liked her even more, knowing she was prepared to work with her tenants should the need arise. And in one of her capacious trunks she'd found breeches, shirt and a leather jerkin that fit him well.

When she stood he said, "Where do they go? The crops. When they are not here, where do they go?"

"I don't understand what you're asking."

"Three years ago, this crop—wheat?—wasn't here."

"Oh. We planted the wheat on the other side of the river. Here, we planted mustard last year and legumes the two years before that. Fallow crops seem to allow the soil to recover from its labors."

"So if I let my fields lie fallow for some period of time, they will recover?"

"Well, there's more to it but, essentially, yes."

"How did you discover this? How did you feed your people when there was no wheat for bread? How did you shelter them without the sheaves to thatch their roofs? How—"

"Stop!" she said, laughing. "We didn't stop growing wheat, we just moved where we grew it. We had the land space, fortunately, to do so. Otherwise, we all would have gone hungry for a time. The hardest part was convincing our people that they wouldn't starve, that the labor of rerouting the river and removing rocks from the soil would be worth all the extra work."

"But you convinced them."

Her lips firmed. Her whole face changed, reminding him that "Willa" meant "resolute" as well as "desired".

"I reminded them that I am the holder of the land and if they wished to remain at Marchonland they would obey me."

"And they did."

She grinned. "Eventually. They grumbled a lot at first. They realized I was serious when my apron full of rocks tumbled me into the river."

"Were you hurt?"

"Only my pride. Then the miller piped up, said he needed a better water flow to the mill and everything got better. After all, 'tis easier to toss stones in the river than it is to move a mill stone by stone.

"But there is something more, isn't there, Vinn?"

"Yes, if I can figure out what to say."

He'd never before seen a solemn smile, but he saw one now.

She said, "A wise lord once told me I had only to ask for what I wanted. He said if it was in his power to give it, he would."

"'That pompous ass! He thought only of sex with you."

"Perhaps, but will he shame me now because I asked for sex and he gave it to me? Will he shame himself because he is too proud to ask for more than sex?"

"No, by damn, he won't! Willa, will you teach me how to do what you do? Will you teach me so that my people won't starve?" He grasped her hands then fell to his knees in the dirt.

"Of course," she said, a tremor in her voice.

He looked up and saw a single tear spill down her cheek. "Willa, I—"

"Oh get up, you fool, before my tears drown you. We need to return to the castle and meet with Aida and Gaspar. We have much to plan and even more to do."

She looked up at him, a hint of hesitation in her turquoise eyes.

"You have only to ask," he reminded her.

"If I can figure out what to say." He kissed her then laughed, a joyous sound she'd heard only when he was buried deep within her. "You don't seem to know much about your land. Is there someone better informed? Someone who can tell me about the soil and the crops and the water?"

"'Twould be best if you saw for yourself. The Eyrie is but three days' ride from here, two if we ride hard. Will you come, Willa? Will you?"

Fear? What could his indomitable Willa fear?

"What is it, dearling?"

"Nothing." Resolve replaced trepidation. "I am not much of a horsewoman, but I will go with you to your Eyrie."

Marchon Castle Stables

Pippa sat on her heels and surveyed mare and foal with a smile of satisfaction.

"She had an easy time of it," Banan said, mirroring Pippa's pose and gazing with awe at the mare and newborn foal.

"For her first birthing, she did amazingly well. You must name the colt. A reward for your assistance," Pippa explained when he looked puzzled. "And as payment for ruining your shirt." He was covered from neck to boots with birthing fluids and blood but didn't seem to mind.

Pippa was dressed in breeches, shirt and jerkin as well. At first, he'd looked appalled by her clothes, but he'd had the sense not to remark. And surely now he could see the reason for her men's garb since she was covered in as much filth as he was.

"I'd rather—" He ran his fingers through his hair, stood with uncharacteristic awkwardness then paced away a few steps. "If you are truly in the mood to offer a reward?"

"I am. But we both stink like pigs, so if tupping is on your mind... No, I can see that isn't what you want. Tell me, Banan."

"No. What I want is too much, well beyond the price of a shirt. Or even a shirt and breeches," he said, looking down at his bloody boots.

"I insist you ask. If I find the price too high I can always say no."

Again he frowned, an expression so foreign to his usual hauteur she found it almost endearing.

"Sirocco. Name the colt Sirocco as a reminder that my lands lie to the south of Marchonland."

"Are you perhaps hoping for a wind to the south? A windfall?"

He blushed—blushed, by damn!—then chuckled. "Am I always so transparent?"

"No, but I like seeing you a little unsure. It helps me to forgive your bossiness."

"The pot calling the kettle black. You, my dear Pippa, are the queen of imperiousness."

"Am I, indeed?" She stroked her chin like a villain in a melodrama then wrinkled her nose, displeased by her own stench. "I order you to muck out this stall then put down fresh straw. Fill the troughs with feed and water. When you've done it all, come back to my tower and I'll reward you with a bath." She stepped closer and stroked his nipples through his ruined shirt. "And other things. After you tell me what you truly want."

Before she could move away, she found herself on her back in muck and straw, Banan on top of her. "Idiot," she laughed. "Let me up."

"Since we both stink like pigs already, why not wallow in the muck before we bathe?"

Laughing harder, she shook her head. "We're disturbing the horses. I'll get some stable boys to clean up in here, but we should move the horses to a clean stall first."

"Afraid of a little hard work, Princess?"

"Are you, Lord Banan?"

He stood then pulled her to her feet. Pippa dug into her shirt.

"Here," she said, holding out a smashed apple. "Mignonette likes apples."

"And carrots," he said, taking the apple from Pippa and holding out both offerings to the mare. The horse and foal followed him to a clean stall. While the mare daintily nibbled from his palm, he reached out to scratch her behind her ears but withdrew his hand without touching her.

"Catch," he said, tossing Pippa a pitchfork and heading back to the birthing stall. Pippa followed and watched as he pitched muck out the stall window into the manure heap outside.

"You've done this before," she said, joining in the effort.

"I've horses at home. None so fine as yours, but of good bloodlines, valiant hearts and strong legs."

Laying her hand on Banan's arm, Pippa said, "Am I that hard to talk to, so unreasonable, you can't even say what you want?"

He swore and flung the pitchfork out the window. "I came here under false pretenses. I didn't want the land. Ravenskeep has land and land and land to spare. I came for—"

"You came for the horses," she said, so softly he barely heard the words. But hear he did, along with the pain behind them.

"Yes, I came for the horses."

"Then you must be congratulated, Lord Banan. You've won. I am not Willa, the holder of the land. I am Pippa, guardian of the horses. You have fucked me and you have won.

"But know this—you will not remove a single horse or foal from Marchonland. If you wish to breed your horses with mine—mine, damn you!—you will bring them here. I will decide if they are worthy. If I deem them unworthy, you will take them back and never bring them to Marchonland again.

"Choose well, Lord Banan, for you will not get a second chance. Ever."

Aida's Tower

Aida gripped Gaspar's hand and squeezed so hard he yelped.

Yvonne curled on the rug near the fire like a contented cat sated by a bowl of cream. For once she'd discarded her chain mail and swords for a simple gown of pale green silk. Her unbound hair flowed down her back as if waiting for a lover's hands.

Willa, dressed as usual in soft blues and creamy white, sat in her usual chair, her lack of serenity betrayed by her restless hands. She too had left her hair unbound, caught at her nape with what appeared to be a man's plain garter.

Pippa prowled from one end of her aunt's solar to the other as if looking for something to break. Everything about her was tense, from her braided hair to her tightly laced jerkin and breeches to her boots.

At last, Aida cleared her throat and said, "Well, nieces, have you been seduced?"

Pippa broke stride long enough to growl and glare. Yvonne stretched languidly. Willa began to chew on her lower lip.

"With varying degrees of satisfaction, it would appear," Gaspar observed, trying to lighten the overall tension.

"I must leave Marchonland," Willa said before the silence became even more unbearable.

Yvonne straightened and looked interested for the first time. Pippa sat as if her legs would no longer hold her. Aida gasped and gripped Gaspar's hand even tighter.

"You can't!" Aida cried.

"That is to say," Gaspar said, taking both of Aida's hands in his before she broke his fingers, "we know of no holder of the land who has ever left Marchonland."

"Why not?" Yvonne said sharply. "Is it forbidden? Will she die if she sets foot outside Marchonland's borders? Will she be banished forever?"

"Stop it, Yvonne. You're frightening your sister to death."

Willa looked pale, but so did Yvonne.

"It is not forbidden, it's only that it's not been done," Aida said in a calmer voice. "If you would tell us why you want to leave, we might better understand."

Willa drew a deep breath then explained how Vinn's people were suffering, how he'd asked for her help, how close his lands were to Marchonland so that she needn't be away for long. "Once we've gotten things going in the right direction," she finished.

"Is that what you want, child?" Gaspar asked gently.

"Yes," Willa said. "I inherited lands that have always been well cared for. Vinn's lands need me. Me." She laughed and hugged herself.

Yvonne stood and placed her hands on Willa's shoulders, seeming to draw strength from the contact. "I must leave as well. Gareth has asked me to train his knights and men-at-arms." She laughed. "Frankly, I think it's a ploy to get me out of my rut, but I have agreed to go with him."

Pippa burst into tears. Her sisters rushed to her side, offering handkerchiefs and comforting pats that only made her cry harder. When she quieted, Aida sat beside her and drew Pippa's head to her shoulder.

"What is it, Pippa, that hurts you so?"

"Banan! The blackguard!" Hiccupping, she swiped at her tears. "Last night he helped me deliver Mignonette's first foal. Last night, covered from head to foot with—well, you know what a birthing stall is like. He didn't seem to mind the mess at all. He even helped me muck it out." Hearing the admiration in her own voice, she sprang to her feet and stormed toward the door then whirled back.

"I let him name the colt, which I never do. 'Twas then that he told me he hadn't come here for the land. He has land out his arse! He doesn't want me, he only wants my horses!" She threw herself into a chair and wailed into her hands.

Willa knelt at Pippa's feet and took her sister's hands. "But, Pippa, you are the horses. You have bred them, raised them, loved them. Each and every one of them. They're as magnificent as they are because of you."

Yvonne headed for the door. "Where is the knave? I'll cut his heart out. No. First I'll geld him then I'll cut out his heart."

"Would you murder the king's cousin?" Gaspar asked from his chair.

Yvonne glared at him. "Fetch the dark green gown for my hanging," she said then focused on her aunt. "I see your hand in this mess."

"I… Yes," Aida said then said nothing more.

"I too had a hand in it, as did your mother," Gaspar added.

"Mother. Of course," Pippa said bitterly.

"Aida and I had no way of knowing who would win the tournament. But once that was settled, we decided which lord should court each of you. That is, should court Willa and Pippa."

"And Gareth? How does the king figure in all of this?"

"He was always meant for you, Yvonne. 'Twas arranged before your birth."

"Pfft!" Yvonne spat, obviously disgusted, although she'd known days earlier.

"Gaspar and I knew Vinn needed Willa's help in returning his lands to prosperity. We knew he was too proud to ask for assistance so—"

"You made it seem as though, if he won my heart, my virginity, he could win my help. Without asking," Willa said, turning away from their intense gazes. Had Vinn lied to her about his feelings? No, not as far as she could remember. Besides, his eyes couldn't lie, not when he was buried in her body and making love to her.

"But he did ask," Gaspar said, "which is what we hoped he would do."

"As for Banan," Aida continued, "we knew he needed to mount more of his knights so that he and Vinn and Gareth could defend themselves and us, should diplomatic doors close."

"Ah," Yvonne said. Pacing to the table, she made a hasty sketch. "'M' is for Marchonland, 'V' for Vinn, 'B' for Banan, 'G' for Gareth. We are in the middle, with Vinn and Banan surrounding us and Gareth surrounding them." She chuckled, a bitter sound, and gestured at the window. "Just as their armies surround us now."

"Banan knew you would not sell your horses willingly, Pippa, if you knew they would be used in battle."

"Even though your destriers were bred and trained for that very purpose," Aida interjected.

"Vinn needs to feed more than his own people, doesn't he? Banan's and Gareth's too."

"Yes."

"Pfft!" the princesses spat in unison.

"And none of them—even you, Aunt Aida, and you, Gaspar—thought to explain this to us."

"Your mother forbade it."

"Ha!" Pippa shouted. "I knew that-that witch had her hands in this. Even from her grave, she hasn't stopped trying to manipulate us!"

"She loved you very much," Aida whispered.

"And she wanted you all to be happy."

"Happy?" Willa said. "How can we be happy, knowing we were duped?"

"Lied to," Yvonne said, fury in her voice.

"Debauched," Pippa muttered then burst into tears. "What have I done? What have I done?"

"What?" asked the others.

"I sent him away. I told him… Oh it doesn't matter what I told him. I sent Banan away and now I'll never know if he even liked me."

"Do you like him?" Yvonne turned from the window and stared at her youngest sister.

"B-before last night, not very much."

"But you did? He didn't?" Aida said, looking fierce. As did Gaspar.

"Rape me? No. He seduced me and…well, last night I thought I could have learned to like him. A little."

"Pfft!" they said together.

"I think," Yvonne began.

"We might even," Willa added.

"Love them," said Pippa, obviously appalled.

"Ahh," said Aida and Gaspar, clasping hands and smiling.

"Don't think you've won," Yvonne said.

"Because you haven't," Pippa added.

"Yet," said Willa, staring at Pippa.

Chapter Ten
Willa's Tower

ဢ

The promise of dawn barely lit Willa's bedchamber. She eased from Vinn's arms and went to sit in the window seat. She couldn't see the fields but she could almost feel them greening, the seeds stretching out of the soil to touch the sun.

She thought of Kerrie holding her hand as they walked row after row, pulling weeds and plucking bugs from tender shoots. Kerrie always seemed to have time, even when Yvonne grew bored and raced away to play with the wooden weapons Gaspar had made for her. And although she could not remember him clearly, she sometimes thought her father Brecc joined them. But it may have been Cesare.

Odd that she would think of those moments now, when she was about to leave Marchonland. Then again, perhaps not so strange. She knew, in her mind, that her people would continue to tend the fields as they always had. And with Gaspar's guidance, they would rotate the crops as Kerrie had taught them. No one would starve unless...

She glanced over at Vinn snuggling her pillow as if it were her body. Where would he be if war broke out before they would prepare his lands to feed his people? Would he leave the task to her, his faith in her still strong? Would she fail him, unable to convince his people of Kerrie's wisdom?

Vinn appeared at her side. Sitting, he drew her onto his lap and pressed her head to his shoulder.

"I should have found another way," he murmured against her forehead. "'Twas unfair of me to ask you to leave your home, your people, your lands."

"I don't mind leaving, Vinn. In fact, I welcome the challenge."

"You won't fail, Willa, if that's what bothers you. Together we can manage any difficulty."

"But if there is war, will we still be together?"

"The king has military men aplenty. He'll be content to leave the war to them while we provision his armies.

She sighed. "So many things can go awry. Too much rain or not enough. Bugs, birds—"

"Mother Nature we cannot control. We can control lazy or doubting tenants."

"Oh?" She wished she felt as confident as he sounded.

"Aye. Simply threaten them with the loss of their ale and they'll obey you."

She laughed and burrowed closer. His words restored her confidence in herself, renewed her belief that, together, they could accomplish anything.

But oh! How she wished for Kerrie's counsel!

* * * * *

Aida's Tower – A Guest Room

"What's wrong?" Vinn asked when Banan, his clothes disheveled, his hair still wet from his morning ablutions, stormed into his chamber without knocking.

"I've been duped, refused, banished," Banan shouted, pouring a tankard of ale and downing it in several long gulps.

"Princess 'Willa' not up to your expectations?" Vinn smiled and stretched his legs toward the cheery fire.

At the subtle emphasis on the princess's name, Banan lunged at Vinn, his fist cocked with all the fury he'd nurtured all night.

"Hold!" Gareth commanded from the door. Closing it behind him, he paced to the table, refilled Banan's tankard and poured two more. Keeping one for himself, he handed the other to Vinn who smiled his thanks. "I sense something is amiss."

"That bastard knew everything and didn't tell me." He threw a glare at Vinn.

"I didn't know," Vinn said reasonably. "I simply guessed those two old dragons had something devious in mind. I managed, not without great difficulty, to befriend Dehy and learned the truth from him."

"What truth?" Banan demanded. He unclenched his fists but flung himself into a chair.

"By 'dragons' I assume you mean Aida and Gaspar," Gareth said mildly.

"And Dehy as well. It seems Dehy has a tendresse for Princess Willa, the real Willa. Not that he doesn't admire Princess Yvonne and Princess Pippa. Ah, I see 'Pippa' means something to you, Banan."

"As Yvonne does to me." The two men stared at Gareth as if they'd like to throttle him. "Go on, Banan. How were you duped, refused and banished?"

"She refused to give me her horses. Told me I could bring mine here, but she would decide if they were worthy—worthy!—of hers. Told me to choose well for I'd not get a second chance."

"Refused and banished," said Vinn.

"That is serious," Gareth said, sitting on Vinn's bed with a sigh.

"And then there was this thing about her name. Insisted I call her Pippa and got all riled up when I called her Willa."

"Ah ha! The duplicitous lie," Vinn drawled.

"Which wasn't a lie at all."

"Well... no. As it turned out it wasn't a lie."

Gareth sighed again, but Vinn was not yet done riling Banan. "You, of course, immediately told Pippa you were after her horses."

"You know I didn't tell her. Until last night, when she forced it from me."

"Forced?" Vinn's eyebrows quirked upward.

"Held a knife to your throat, did she?" Gareth asked, joining in the teasing.

"No! She just kept asking me, over and over. What did I want? What did I want? So I told her that I came to Marchonland for the horses. And that's when she..." He shrugged and threw the tankard against the wall, showering Vinn with ale.

Sputtering, Vinn surged from his chair and lunged.

Gareth stepped between them and withstood their blows. Glaring at him, they slunk back to their chairs.

"Didn't it even occur to you to say that you love her?" Gareth said softly.

"And compound the lie?"

"Then you not only lost the horses, you lost the chance to—"

"Tup her? No, that's the one area in which I succeeded."

"And?" Gareth and Vinn prompted.

Laughing, running his fingers through his rumpled hair, Banan said, "She seemed to like that well enough. No, I'm sure she liked it. I wish I were as certain she liked me."

Slapping Banan's shoulder, Gareth said, "Women have always liked you."

"Not this one. She's haughty, argumentative, prickly as a porcupine and—"

"In short, just like you," Vinn jibed.

Gareth stroked his chin then said, "I think the question here is do you like her well enough to beg?"

"Beg?" Banan said, his voice rising with incredulity.

"Crawl on your knees if need be." Vinn laced his fingers behind his head and grinned at his cousins.

"I won't!"

"You shall," Gareth said, assuming his most royal posture. "You shall and she shall forgive you for everything. If necessary, I'll order her to marry you."

"Good luck trying to order Pippa to do anything," Banan muttered.

"You aren't king here," Vinn added.

"Meaning you are?" Gareth asked, his voice low and deadly. "Have you and Willa married? Has she given you her authority to rule as holder of the land, keeper of her people?"

"No," Vinn said cautiously. Gareth had the power to forbid the marriage, a thought Vinn found unsettling. He wanted Willa as his wife.

"Then I suggest you see Willa and, between the two of you, devise a means to get Pippa to talk to Banan. And you," he pointed at Banan, "figure out what you're going to say when you see Pippa."

"Don't you mean if?" Banan said, reverting to his usual lordly sneer.

"Think, damn you!" Gareth bellowed. "And plan on crawling."

"Where are you going? Don't tell me you're going to that virago, Aida!"

"No, I'm going to see Yvonne and beg her—I, your king—will beg her to intercede with Pippa on your haughty, arrogant, prickly behalf." He slammed the door behind him.

"Whew!" Vinn swiped his brow and shook the sweat from his fingers. "I've never seen Gareth in such a temper. Not even with Gerard and Edgar."

"He's right to be pissed. Those horses are too important to let—"

"I suggest you stop thinking about the horses and concentrate on Pippa." Vinn slammed the door behind him.

Banan paced the length and breadth of Vinn's room. "'Pippa, sweeting.' No. God no! 'Pippa, dearling, I…' She'll never buy it. Or these clothes. I'll wear the white doublet with the red— No, she didn't like those clothes. Or me in them for that matter. Damn!"

He paced another circle of Vinn's chamber. Arriving at the window, he peered out and spotted a corner of the stables. Last night, even covered with muck and stinking like a pigsty she'd seemed to like him—a little.

"Ahh," he said and smiled. Neither the clothes he'd burned last night, nor the clothes he'd worn when he first met her, but a less odoriferous version of last night. And a prayer that he'd not offend her. Again.

"Pippa, my love…" he began then started. Damn it, he meant it! Even if she demanded he crawl on his belly, he would do it. Not for Gareth and the horses, but because he loved her. Loved her! he thought, searching for dismay, reluctance, pride. Anything that would allow him to spurn her and retain his dignity.

He couldn't find any excuse. Whistling, he left Vinn's room and quietly shut the door behind him.

Chapter Eleven
Pippa's Tower

ॐ

"No, no, no, no. No! I don't want to see him. I won't!"

"Pippa, you saw my sketch," Yvonne said, striving for patience but finding none. "You know what's at stake."

"If you don't accept him, Marchonland, all of it, will be lost!"

"That's a lie, Willa! Yet another lie in a long list of lies. Yvonne will defend us. To the death if necessary. And you, Willa, will ensure our people, all our people—even Banan's—will be fed. We will outlast every enemy, even if we must stand alone, without Vinn or Gareth or B-Banan."

"You're wrong, Pippa," Yvonne said, her voice betraying her weariness. "I'll not be here to defend Marchonland. I shall be at Gareth's side, defending his land and his people and Vinn's and Banan's as well. Because defending them is Marchonland's best and only defense."

"Nor will I be here," Willa said. "I shall be with Vinn's people, harvesting his crops, feeding his people, slaughtering his horses to feed all our armies," she added, her voice menacing, knowing she used the threat against Pippa's love for her horses. But she knew she would slaughter the horses if it meant their armies could fight on.

"Pfft!" Pippa spat. "You have already surrendered Marchonland. Surrendered it to tupping. Just like Kerrie did!"

"For God's sake—"

"For all our sakes! For your horses' sake if nothing else!"

"At least see Banan."

"Hear him out."

"Listen with your heart, since your hearing has fled already."

"You don't have to forgive him," Willa said, chaffing Pippa's icy hands.

"Not immediately. Or not at all," Yvonne amended, seeing Pippa's glare.

Pippa sighed then said, "Don't you want to punish the others? Gareth and Vinn?"

Yvonne and Willa glanced at each other then shook their heads.

"But we'll help you"

"Punish Banan, if you must."

"So long as you forgive him at the end."

"After making him grovel."

"Banan grovel? Never!" Pippa said, folding her arms over her chest.

"I'll wager he will," Yvonne said, laying her favorite jewel-encrusted dagger on Pippa's table.

"As will I," Willa said, stripping off her fanciest garters and silk hose and adding them to Yvonne's offering. "What will you wager, Pippa? Besides your heart?"

"I'll never give Banan my heart."

Her sisters merely smiled knowingly.

"Oh very well. I'll wager Sirocco's first foal that Banan won't grovel."

"You expect us to wait at least three years for you to pay your debt?"

"'Twill be worth the wait. Think on it, Willa. Sirocco as sire, Banan's best mare as dam. Already my purse grows heaving with our racing winnings."

Looking at her younger sister, Willa said, "No cheating, Pippa. You'll not breed Sirocco to some dray mare in order to renege. Agreed?"

Pippa eyed them both then said, "If Banan grovels, I give my word you two shall have Sirocco's first foal. If Banan does not grovel, Willa will embroider a new pair of garters for me and Yvonne will teach me how to use her new most favored dagger.

"Don't argue, Yvonne. You change your mind about your favorite weapon as easily as you change your gowns. And you, Willa, change your embroidery designs as readily. I'll have new from both of you or all bets are cancelled. Agreed?"

Her sisters nodded.

Pippa smiled. "Now define 'grovel'."

"Just like our mother," Willa said and heaved an overwrought sigh.

"Too devious for words," Yvonne said, shaking her head and looking grievously disappointed.

"Grovel," Pippa repeated.

"Crawling."

"On his knees."

"On his belly," Pippa said. "Agreed?"

"Agreed," said her sisters, shaking hands then leaving her with only her thoughts for company.

I am no better than my mother, Pippa thought. She was disgusted by how much she missed having Banan in her arms, his cock buried deep in her cunt, both of them racing toward completion. Their first coupling of the day always seemed as though they couldn't wait to reach those heights.

But sometimes Banan would make her wait. He'd lick, stroke, suck until she thought she'd go mad, she craved release so badly. He knew, damn him, when she neared her peak, was about to soar to ecstasy, needed to have him in her to take that final step.

He'd suggest a game of chance, or a bath, or a visit to the stables. Then he'd coax her to sit on his lap. She could feel his cock grow and pulse and the need, that fire he kindled with his lightest caress, grew until it didn't matter where they were or who was around. She had to have him.

Was this how Kerrie felt when Pippa's father touched her? Had she felt the same with Alexandre and Brecc? Had she wanted every man who touched her?

Could I take Vinn into my body? she wondered, remembering how everything about him frightened her. She, who faced horses in a frenzy to mate without trepidation, cringed at the very thought of the dark lord's hands on her. The thought of him driving into her left her shivering with revulsion.

Was Banan the only man who could make her want until she ached with need? Would she, like Kerrie, spend her life searching for that perfect joining? Or would she pass the rest of her life alone?

Dear God! Did she love Banan?

Chapter Twelve
Yvonne's Tower

&

"How do you know you love me, Yvonne?"

"Did I say I love you? If so, I don't remember so it doesn't count."

Gareth folded his arms over his chest and frowned at her. "How?" he repeated, looking like Solomon must have looked when he threatened the baby with his sword. "You have taken three of us into your body, so how can you say you love me?"

Resigned to telling him the truth, she said, "You said it yourself, Gareth. 'Even truly blind' I would know you."

Struggling to find the words that would soften his fierce expression, she worried her lower lip with her teeth. Passion flared in his dark eyes. For a moment she considered using his desire for her to persuade him of her love but cast the thought aside. Kerrie would have used that lust to force her will on the man she desired, Yvonne knew she had to find another way to convince Gareth.

But how? She had no model other than Kerrie to use.

But I do, she thought, feeling a little hopeful. Aida and Gaspar had been in love for years and years. What kept them together? More than lust, certainly, although everyone in Marchonland knew the two still lusted for each other.

"Perhaps," Yvonne began then shook her head. No equivocation, she told herself. "I could hate—no, not ever hate but certainly dislike you for your role in this charade we've all been playing at for weeks."

"Likewise," he said with a "so what?" grin. "I didn't enlist in the tournament and pretend to be a man."

"You didn't enlist in the tournament at all," she reminded him, hoping her expression conveyed just how cowardly she thought him.

"I had neither need nor desire to win your sister. Either of them."

"Oh," she said in a small voice. "Still, all five of you men came to Marchonland under false pretenses."

"Not entirely. Gerard and Edgar did compete in the tournament but lost to you, who in turn lost to Vinn and Banan. But you stall, Yvonne. Forget the pretexts and tell me why you think you love me."

She glared at him. "Were I my mother—"

"Which you aren't," he interrupted, looking pleased that she wasn't Kerrie.

"Pfft!" Yvonne thought for a moment then blurted out, "You respect me, as I respect you." He shot her an interested look that encouraged her to continue. "The other day on the training grounds, you could have let me defeat you, but you didn't. Unlike Edgar and Gerard, you gave me your best."

Gareth, looking uncomfortable, shifted his feet. "Yes, well, my brothers have much to learn about women—especially stubborn ones," he added, rubbing his shoulder where she'd landed a wicked blow with the flat of her sword. Casting her a sardonic look, he said, "Lust and respect. Is there more? Do you, for example, find me more handsome than my brothers or my cousins?"

"You are all handsome men," she said, answering his scowl with a grin. "But there is something in you, a darkness I want to ease."

"I am not a child, Yvonne. I don't need coddling."

"Need, no. But you sometimes want it. So do I," she admitted with a sigh. "Being the eldest can be a burden. Kerrie was always caught up in her own wants. And Aida—bless her!—kept trying to ensure all our needs were met but as the eldest it fell to me to be 'Mother' more often than I wanted."

"We can share tears for our lost childhoods."

"Yes," she said, knowing he gave her sarcasm in lieu of sincerity. "And we can share laughter over escapades, both ours and our siblings' that went awry. That is what I want for you, Gareth. Love and respect. Lust and laughter."

"As I want for you." He looked like he might say something about loving her, but he chuckled.

"What? What's going through that devious mind of yours?"

"Now that I'm satisfied you truly love me, Yvonne, my love, help me reconcile Pippa and Banan."

"I will. After you explain why, when that creature—"

"The putrid pustule?"

She shot him an impatient glance. "—came calling, you let me handle him until help arrived. I am most interested in why you stayed in the background then."

Gareth had wanted to avoid this conversation, but he knew Yvonne would keep at him until he told her the truth. Squaring his shoulders, he took her hand and led her to the window seat. She sat, he paced.

"I could claim a noble intent—this is your land to rule as you must. While we both know that's true, it is not the entire truth." He sighed, paced away then returned to face her squarely. "The rest of the truth is I was afraid. Afraid to reveal myself as king. That's why, when my men cried out 'To the king,' Edgar, Gerard and I all stepped forward."

"Do you know how frightened I was? That horrible man could have been the king and your men could have been coming to his aid."

"Did you truly believe I would betray you? That I would use him to gain access to your secret passages and would use them to enter Marchon Castle and claim it for my own?"

Her gaze slid from his face to the floor. What seemed an eternity later she looked up at him. "I think I knew you wouldn't." She placed her hand over her heart. "Here, I believed in you. But here," she tapped her forehead, "I doubted all of you.

"I thought I would have to kill him and then face my own death. 'Tis a most unpleasant thought at any time, but I think—" She drew a deep breath to calm her heart that raced like it had that night when she'd confronted the pretender. "I hope I would have risked it."

"Why?"

"Because he was evil. Because I sensed in him not only disrespect for all women but for every living thing. He would have destroyed Marchonland and blamed my mother. Then he would have gone on to destroy Puttupon and Eyrie and Ravenskeep and blamed your father."

She chuckled, a self-deprecating sound. "Not that all of that occurred to me while I was standing there. But later, when Aida confirmed he was dead—I thought he had died because of me. Ha! Vanity at its ignoble best. He died because of what he was, what he had done, what he would do. I'm not sorry he is dead. And what does it say about me, that I wish I had killed him myself?"

Gareth sat beside her and took her hands. "It says you're human. 'Tis never easy to take a life, especially when that life is of your own blood."

"I'm sorry it fell to you to do so."

He shook his head. "It had to be done. I should have done it long before now. But there are no books of instruction about being a ruler. We learn as we go and we sometimes make mistakes." He drew her to him and gently kissed her lips. "Now will you help me with Pippa and Banan?"

Smiling up at him, she nodded. "As soon as you tell me why you love me."

Gareth cleared his throat.

Yvonne thought he looked like he'd rather face the chopping block than say the words she longed to hear. She didn't need those words. Just like Kerrie hadn't needed to hear Brecc say them when they said their vows, Yvonne didn't need the words. But she wanted them. She wanted to hear Gareth say them, to know she could die with the words and the memory of them in Garth's voice filling her mind when she drew her final breath.

"I admire you, Yvonne."

"Uh huh," she prompted when his gaze focused somewhere behind her. "What do you admire, Gareth?"

"Well…" He sucked a breath then said in a rush, "I admire your courage. For example, you could have retreated when William threatened you."

She fixed a politely interested expression on her face and waited for him to continue.

"You are beautiful. Yes, beautiful." Nodding as if pleased by that description, he sat beside her and took her hand. "You-you are the most skillful warrior I have ever faced."

"Courageous. Beautiful. Skillful. And you admire me for these traits?"

"Yes. And damn it, Yvonne! I'm no bard who can compose a ballad to tell you how I feel."

"I know that, Gareth. And I know you enjoy our tupping. I enjoy it too. But what will happen when we're older than Aida and Gaspar are now? When we focus on the cares of the day more than we focus on each other? When our children are grown and there's no one to talk to except each other? What then, Gareth?"

He looked into her eyes and she could see in his the future they would build together. Both of them wrinkled, stooped, a little forgetful of minute details but not forgetful of this. This love that bound them at this moment. This love that would bind them all their lives.

"I love you, Yvonne. 'Tis as simple and complicated as that."

"Aye," she said, raising her head to receive his kiss. "As simple as that."

Willa's Tower

"What are we going to do about Pippa and Banan?" Willa asked. She sat in her favorite chair, plucking at the age-yellowed lace surrounding her mother's bridal bouquet.

"I wish I knew," Vinn said, smoothing his hair but only messing it even more.

"I wish Banan could admit he loves her, but I suppose that's impossible. He doesn't seem the kind of man—"

"You've met Banan? When? Where?"

Frowning at Vinn's belligerent tone, Willa said, "In Pippa's tower, the night before I met you." Taking Vinn's silence as a prompt to continue, she went on. "Dehy told me Pippa needed to see me, he didn't know why. So I went to Pippa's tower and Banan appeared in all his snooty splendor."

She smoothed her satin skirts then looked up at Vinn. "I'd just returned from the fields and—"

"I knew there was something different about you that first morning."

"Pardon?"

"That night, the night you met Banan, I believe I met Pippa. She seemed terrified of me. But that morning, the morning I met you, you wondrous Willa, seemed completely unafraid. You even seemed to like me more than somewhat." He stroked her cheek and placed a soft kiss on it.

Feeling a blush stealing over her chest and face, she lowered her head and sniffed the faded roses. "I did—I do like you." She looked up at him. "I think Aida and Gaspar had a hand in those chance meetings."

Shaking his head but smiling, Vinn said, "I agree and ordinarily I'd recommend we do something to discourage their meddling. Given the situation with your sister and my cousin, I'm afraid Aida and Gaspar will have to wait for their punishment."

He paced away then turned back. "I don't understand, Willa, how you and Yvonne can forgive us for what must seem an unconscionable betrayal."

"Frankly, neither can I. When we realized all of you wanted something more than tupping, we were all furious. But Yvonne and I realized what Pippa is unwilling to admit. Not yet anyway."

"Oh?" Quirking a brow, Vinn led Willa to the window seat then sat beside her.

"We tried to trick you. Pippa and Yvonne competed in the tournament but you and Banan bested them."

"Ahh. No wonder you fainted when—"

"Pippa."

" — was unhorsed."

Willa bristled and withdrew her hand from his. "She could have been killed."

"Yes, as Yvonne could have been killed when I struck her sword from her hand. But we digress. Do you think you could persuade Pippa to see Banan? Willa?" he said, tipping her chin and making her look at him.

"I think Pippa will see Banan, perhaps even listen to what he has to say but I promised Pippa that Banan would grovel. Yvonne and I wagered that Banan would crawl on his belly. In truth, I cannot imagine him on his knees let alone on his belly."

"Not in public, certainly."

"Pippa will fib to win the bet she made with Yvonne and me. We must have witnesses to what happens between them."

"Damn!"

"But we didn't say we had to see him grovel. We could hear him and her."

"From where? The Eyrie has many listening posts but I know of none here."

"There is at least one that I know of. In Aida's tower. She and Kerrie used to keep track of us from Aida's tower."

"You mean that harridan? Your aunt heard everything we said and did?"

He looked so appalled Willa couldn't help laughing. "I doubt Aunt Aida heard much of anything. Gaspar — "

"Heard as well? Shit! Is nothing sacred around here?"

"As I started to say, I'm sure Gaspar has kept my aunt thoroughly distracted all week. And Yvonne swears Kerrie wouldn't eavesdrop on intimate moments."

"Then, if I understand correctly, we could listen to Banan grovel, but we need not hear him or her or them when he—"

"If he convinces her to forgive him. By whatever means he, she, they choose."

Grabbing her hand, Vinn pulled her to her feet and rushed toward the door.

"Hold," she demanded, sounding so much like Gareth that Vinn stopped in mid-stride.

"What? What now?" Impatience showed in both voice and visage.

"First, Yvonne and I must convince Aida and Gaspar that spying on Pippa and Banan is necessary."

"Their reconciliation is paramount. If any of us is to be happy, we must reconcile those two."

"I agree, but Aida and Gaspar don't know that we know about the listening post in Aida's tower. More important, Pippa does know about it and about our knowing."

"Shit!" he said again with greater vehemence. "Now what do we do?"

Willa took back her hand and, lost in thought, returned to the window seat. At last she looked up. "Yvonne and I must attend Pippa until Banan arrives. Once he's with her, we can make our excuses and join you and Gareth in Aida's tower."

"Won't Pippa think it strange that you and Yvonne leave just when you're about to win your bet? Or not win it."

"At that point I don't think Pippa will notice anything except Banan."

Vinn sat beside Willa and again took her hand. His thumb caressed her palm and she shivered with anticipation. If only they had time, right now, to bring each other to fulfillment, she thought, stroking his cheek. His dark eyes flashed desire then filled with an emotion she'd never seen before. An odd pressure formed around her heart and tears stung her eyes.

"You know I love you, Willa. Don't you?"

He kissed her gently, fleetingly, as he had kissed her the first time. That kiss, even more than the words, convinced her he spoke the truth.

"I love you too," she whispered and leaned against him. This quiet satisfaction, simply being together, must be what had kept Aida and Gaspar together for so many years. Willa sighed and sat up straight. "We must see Yvonne and Gareth then convince Aida and Gaspar to help us."

"I suppose we must," Vinn said, sounding like he'd rather face a hostile army.

"You'll not go unrewarded," she said. "I promise."

Laughing, Vinn kissed her hand and tucked it into the crook of his arm. "I like the sound of that."

Pippa's Tower

When Banan appeared in the doorway between Pippa's solar and bedchamber, she shot a killing look at her two companions then turned that deadly gaze on him. He barely noticed the other women slip by him. He couldn't take his eyes off Pippa. For the first time since he'd met her, she looked like a princess.

Her braided hair lay coiled atop her head, held in place by gem-encrusted combs. She wore a gown of molasses-colored fabric that matched her tawny eyes and its square, low-cut neckline revealed the generous curves of her breasts. She literally stole his breath. But the stormy expression in her eyes told him he'd need more than words to show her he thought her beautiful and he loved her.

He kept his gaze on her face and knelt in the doorway.

Her glare changed, first to confusion then to absolute horror.

"What are you doing?" she squeaked.

On his hands and knees he crept toward her then glanced up. She looked even more horrified, dashing his hopes that this kind of humiliation would satisfy her need for revenge. Sighing, he lowered himself to his belly and shimmied across the floor. When he reached the middle of the room he raised his head and discovered she had retreated several paces.

Groaning inwardly, he again lowered his chest to the floor.

"What are you doing?" she said, again sounding panicked. "Get up, damn it! Damn, damn, damn! You've lost me the bet. Oh pfft, pfft, pfft! I've lost Sirocco's first foal b-because…"

She buried her face in her hands and, wailing, raced to her window seat. There, she struggled to open the window. When it seemed the window would not obey her repeated demands to open, she stood on the window seat and pummeled the glass.

Banan, fearing she would succeed in her quest then throw herself out the open casement and onto the slate roof, roared at her to stop. As easily as Gareth had stopped Banan's assault on Vinn, Pippa stayed her fist, wobbled and then obligingly tipped into his arms.

He sat on the window seat with Pippa on his lap. He handed her his handkerchief, hoping it would quiet her tears, but she cried all the harder.

"Pippa, dearling," he began only to yelp when she slapped him. He caught her hands, prepared to tie them if he must to make her listen to reason.

Surprising him, she pressed gentle kisses on his sore cheek then looked up at him. Her eyes still held tears, but to him those tears looked like dewdrops on amber honey.

"May I ask a question, Pippa? Without you slapping me again?"

"I cannot promise I won't hit you again but ask your question and I'll do my best not to let temper rule me."

He wanted to ask about the wager and losing Sirocco's first foal but thought it wiser to focus on her. "May I kiss you?"

"You've never asked before," she said, looking suspicious of his motives.

"I've never felt this way before."

"Pfft!"

She looked even less inclined to believe whatever he might say. He kissed her and let the gentleness tell her that he cherished her, desired her, needed her more than he needed his next breath. Releasing her hands, he prayed she would touch him. Anywhere. Everywhere. Desire and joy surged through him when she ran her fingers through his hair and deepened the kiss.

He wanted to rip away their clothes and bury himself deep inside her. Instead, he eased her away.

Her eyes drifted open, eyes glazed with a desire that matched his own.

"We need to talk," she began then pressed her lips to his. Leaning against his chest, she drew him down until they lay, his legs tangled with hers, her heartbeat matching his, the staccato like two horses racing for home.

"When we're together like this I can barely think, let alone talk."

"Neither can I but…" She sighed then pushed at his shoulders.

He sat up but kept her near, his arm around her narrow waist, her head on his shoulder. Her fingers traced from his jaw to his nipple and he bit back a groan.

"Tell me about Lord Vinn," she murmured, still caressing him.

Banan felt like she'd pushed him into an icy stream. He grabbed her shoulders and held her at arms' length. "What has Vinn to do with anything? With us?"

She shoved away his hands then stood and glared down at him. "When I asked if you knew him, you looked and sounded as if you didn't like him."

"I don't but he's my cousin. We fostered under Gareth's father at Puttupon Castle."

"Hmmm."

Banan didn't know what to think about "hmmm" in lieu of "pfft". He suspected he should not feel hopeful, but he hated feeling anxious and jealous.

"What does 'hmmm' mean, Pippa?"

"It means I want to meet him, Banan. I was promised a choice and I intend to have it."

"This is your revenge, isn't it? Because I told you the truth—"

"When I forced it from you."

"You're punishing me."

"You lied!"

"Yes, I lied. But know this, Pippa." He grabbed her arm and spun her into him. She looked like she wanted to hit him again, he gripped her hands until she winced and quit fighting him.

"I won't let you go, Pippa. You are mine, mine alone. I'll let no other have you. No other will ever touch you, taste you, drive his cock into your cunt until you scream his name. Forever, I shall hear my name on your lips. Banan, the name you screamed the first time you came and every time thereafter. My name and my name only."

"You left me no choice! You robbed me of my virtue and raped my choice."

"Pippa." He willed his voice to cajole, seduce. "Sweet, tasty, responsive Pippa. Do you truly want to let him touch you, taste you, fuck you and bring you to ecstasy?"

"Mayhap not. But thanks to you, I no longer have a choice."

"Thanks to me, you will not have to suffer his touch."

"Pfft! The choice was supposed to be mine. Not yours, mi—!"

Aida's Tower

"Sounds to me like he has his tongue down her throat," Gaspar observed wryly.

"He has something down her throat," Aida snapped, pushing a lever that closed off all sounds from Pippa's tower.

Yvonne looked at Willa then each looked at Gareth and Vinn. Together they expelled a collective sigh and smiled. It seemed Aida and Gaspar were not voyeurs, at least not with others present.

"Now what?" Gareth said.

Yvonne took his hand and squeezed it gently. "Now we must arrange for Pippa to meet Vinn."

"We have met," said Vinn, slipping his arm around Willa's waist and drawing her to his side.

"As you," Willa pointed accusingly at Aida and Gaspar, "well know. If she changes her mind about Banan and now wants Vinn I'll have Yvonne do something horrible to her."

"She won't want me," Vinn reassured her. "I told you, she's terrified of me."

"Make sure she stays that way!" Willa yelled then said in a lower voice, "We should warn Banan."

"No!" Aida and Gaspar said in unison.

Gaspar continued. "Banan must truly believe Pippa might choose Vinn over him."

"His actions, more than any words, will convince Pippa that he loves her. Or doesn't," Aida added under her breath.

"I want my sword," Vinn demanded. "I won't give Banan a chance to kill me over Pippa."

The other five shouted, "No!"

"Yvonne will protect you, Cousin."

Looking surprised but pleased, Yvonne kissed Gareth's cheek.

"If Kerrie wasn't dead already, I'd kill her," Aida said to the room at large.

"Why?" Gaspar said, twining his fingers through hers. "All her—our—girls will be happy. Which is what we all want." He nodded at Yvonne and Willa who each clung to her lover.

"From your lips," Aida began.

"To yours," Gaspar finished and kissed her.

After some discussion they all agreed on a plan and adjourned.

Alone at last, Gaspar took Aida in his arms and kissed her soundly. "No more worrying, love."

"'Tis easy for you to say." Aida pushed from his arms and went to a small chest atop a table. She withdrew her sister's will and, with Gaspar reading over her shoulder, scanned Kerrie's testament.

She gasped then moaned.

"What?" Concerned, Gaspar took the parchment from her shaking hands and sat with her on his lap.

"Read the part about Pippa. 'So I wish for all my daughters.' Did Kerrie mean they must all be seduced before they married? Or did she wish only that they all be happy in their marriages? Was Pippa the only one to be seduced or—?"

Gaspar kissed her quiet. "Does it matter?" he murmured against her ear. "They've all been seduced. They will all be happy."

"Even Pippa?" she asked in a small voice quite unlike her own.

Gaspar chuckled. "Perhaps Pippa most of all, since she's had the most difficult challenge of all of our girls."

"How so?" Aida sighed and, tilting her head, presented her neck for him to kiss.

"Can you imagine loving Gareth or Vinn or both?"

"Easily," she whispered.

"And can you imagine loving Banan?"

"Merciful heaven, no!"

"Well then," Gaspar said and, together, they laughed.

Chapter Thirteen

℘

Vinn had spent an hour preparing for the confrontation between himself, Banan and Pippa. Although he'd had no sword, he'd limbered his body with thrusts and parries, which for the first time in a week did not include Willa. He now felt comfortable in his own body and quite prepared to fight his rival to the death. Well, Banan's death at any rate. Vinn had too much to live for to die now.

Sterne, Vinn's valet, finally had been allowed into the castle. He'd brought Vinn fresh clothes and had given him the first totally decent shave he'd had in over a week. Now, shaved, bathed, refreshed, all he needed was Willa at his side.

But no. For this to work, Pippa must believe Vinn wanted her and only her.

* * * * *

Banan returned to Pippa's chamber to find Aida shouting orders like a field general. "Turn the mattress." "Dust the tables and chairs." "Someone find Portier to have the tub removed."

"Where is Pippa?" he demanded, his voice lost in the din of maids' chatter. Unaccustomed to being ignored, he shouted the question.

Aida turned and scowled up at him, shooing a maid with her hands. The maid, eyes lowered, brushed by him, nearly tumbling him backward into the tub of soapy water, a tub he and Pippa had shared every morning since they first made love.

Nay, 'twasn't love he felt for her but lust. He knew differently but wasn't about to admit it again. Even to himself. But he could admit to feeling anxiety, this rage that she might choose that— He had no description vile enough to describe Vinn. That she might choose Vinn over him infuriated him. He had won her body. Why, then, did it seem so important to win her heart?

"I believe you'll find Pippa in the great hall, Lord Banan," said Aida, looking as though he were a particularly distasteful bug she longed to squash.

"Thank you," he said and, not knowing why, made a deep bow to her.

For a moment she gazed up at him, her mouth agape. Then she smiled and he felt as if she'd blessed him.

Marchon Castle Great Hall

Aida watched Vinn and Banan glare at each other as they paced through the doors to the great hall. She suspected they would have drawn swords, if they'd had them, and hacked each other to pieces. She almost shouted for the men-at-arms, but seeing the girl in the Princess Chair, decided to let her deal with the men's tempers. No one in the entire castle was so well-equipped to deal with warring factions.

Banan raced toward the dais. Vinn hesitated only a moment then sped after his rival. Just as they each reached out to grab her, the girl stood, a short sword in each hand. Aida squelched a laugh as the men's gazes shifted between each other, the swords and finally, the girl's face.

"What have you done to Pippa?" Lord Banan asked in a low voice full of menace.

"Yes. What have you done with Pippa?" Lord Vinn bellowed.

My, my, my, Aida thought, how things have changed. Lord Vinn, normally so polite as to seem obsequious, bellowing like a bull? Was this part of the pretense or had he forgotten what they'd agreed to last night?

And what about demanding Lord Banan, a week ago a self-centered prig, now asking first about his lady?

"Back away from my woman," Gareth demanded from behind Aida's back while Edgar and Gerard advanced a pace.

"Yours am I, Gareth? Just when did you decide that?" Yvonne said.

Her question went unanswered. Willa grasped the hand that threatened Vinn while Pippa stood between Yvonne and Banan.

"My God, there are three of them!" Banan squeaked. "I suspected there might be two but...three?"

"And they all look alike. Exactly alike," said Vinn. He'd noticed the similarity between Willa and Yvonne, but that three of them should look nearly identical was more than he could absorb all at once.

Willa wore a turquoise gown shot with gold threads. The color matched her glorious eyes, eyes that seemed to reflect the diamonds gleaming in her gold coronet. Eyes that reminded him this was a charade meant to convince Pippa that she wanted Banan, not Vinn.

He took Pippa's hand and drew her away from Banan. In typical Banan fashion, he bristled but was restrained by Gerard and Edgar. Vinn paced around her, a considering expression on his face. He imagined himself buying a horse and coughed to cover his laugh.

In truth, in her gown of brown and gold, she was nearly as beautiful as Willa. Nearly. She was too slender for his tastes and lacked Willa's graceful curves. And even though she had requested this meeting, her expression told him she did not relish his scrutiny.

He glanced at Yvonne and saw her quick smile. Tonight, she wore green, the cut of her gown revealing nicely rounded breasts and a narrow waist. Attractive, yes, but he felt no interest in her beyond admiration. His body didn't ready for her warmth as it did when he looked at Willa.

Yvonne frowned and he returned his attention to Pippa. He touched her cheek, she cringed away. That, if nothing else, should tell her where her affections truly lay.

"They could be triplets," he said, looking at each in turn.

"Except for the eyes," Gareth said, pacing to Yvonne, a look of wonder on his face. Fearless, he took the swords from Yvonne's hands and gave them to his brothers.

"We could have changed places," Willa muttered, disgust in her voice.

"At any time," Pippa added, facing Lord Banan, her hands on her hips.

"And none of you would have known the difference," Yvonne finished, plopping down in the Princess Chair then wincing. Damn, but her ass was tender.

"All cats…"

"In the dark…"

"Howl the same."

Five male voices chorused various denials, Willa and Pippa stared open-mouthed at Yvonne. "Three? You had all three?"

Tilting her chin, Yvonne said defiantly, "Swallowing is a little difficult with a cock in your mouth and the ass-fucking hurt a little at first, but I truly enjoyed having Gareth's cock in my cunt. In fact, I enjoyed all of them and everything we did together." She glared at Gareth as if he intended to banish her to the nursery without any toys.

"In truth, Yvonne," Gerard began.

"'Tis our fault Gareth—"

"You're only making it worse, Edgar." Going down on one knee at Yvonne's feet, Gareth looked up at her and took her hands in his. "I love you, Yvonne."

"And I love you."

Edgar and Gerard elbowed each other and laughed.

"But I l-like them too."

Gareth stood. Whispering into her ear, he vowed, "I'll mouth-fuck you, ass-fuck you or cunt-fuck you anytime, anywhere, you please."

Her face radiant, Yvonne smiled up at him then said, "But can you do all three at once, Gareth?"

He laughed and drew her to him. "Not at precisely the same time, but I'm sure we can work out something."

Pulling on Banan's hand, Pippa whispered, "I understand the mouth and cunt thing but—"

"Mouth and ass?" Willa said, looking at Vinn as if her teacher had left out several important lessons.

"Yes, mouth and ass and cunt. Had I known you might enjoy all three..." He shrugged then captured her hand. "Come with me. We'll work on those lessons together."

"Not just yet, Vinn."

"There's still a matter of choice here, Banan."

"I love you, Pippa. I don't care about the horses, I only care—"

"You had better care about my horses, Banan, for they'll be ours."

"About you. I didn't mean to or want to but— Oh shit!" he said, seeing Pippa's expression change from adoration to anger.

"Didn't mean to love me? Didn't want to love me? Pfft! I don't want a man who—"

"Loves you with all his heart." Kneeling, he caught her hands, kissed them, then lowered his chest to the floor.

"Not again," Pippa groaned. "Get up, Banan. Please."

"Not until you admit you love me."

"Oh all right! I love you but—"

Banan sprang to his feet and kissed her soundly.

"I still intend to look at all of you men before I make my choice."

"Don't even think about Gareth. He's mine," Yvonne warned, stepping in front of him and crossing her arms under her breasts.

"Spoil sport!"

Willa and Pippa circled Vinn and Banan who withstood the scrutiny with resignation.

Pippa said of Vinn, "He's far too dark, too tall, too much of everything."

Surveying Banan, Willa said, "Not for me—Vinn, I mean. But this one—pfft!"

Then each stood before her chosen partner and reached out to cup him.

"Not here!" Banan said, blushing to the roots of his blond hair.

"Not now," Vinn cautioned, casting an embarrassed glance around the hall.

Yvonne cooed, "What do you call it, Gareth, when everyone does everybody?"

"An orgy. And we aren't having one. I'm done sharing you with anyone."

As the three couples made their way toward their respective towers, Edgar said to Aida, "How is it that the princesses look alike?"

"Same mother, different fathers. Kerrie, their mother, put her seal on them and they all look like her," Gaspar explained.

Gerard and Edgar chuckled, only now realizing why Yvonne had laughed so heartily at the three of them.

"Except for their eyes," Aida added. "Those colors came from their fathers."

Slinging one arm around Gaspar's shoulders and the other around Aida's waist, Gerard asked, "Do you know any more intriguing ladies in the neighborhood?"

"Maybe two or three," Gaspar replied.

"There are twins a week's hard ride away," Aida said. Looking at Gerard and Edgar in turn, she saw them smile at each other.

"I've heard they've not yet been f—" Gaspar began.

Aida poked him. "We've had enough of those words."

"The twins are hellions I'm told. But I'd wager they'd be up for an orgy."

Enjoy an excerpt from:
SWORD AND CROWN

Jaac Sarne looked into the face of the only woman he'd ever loved and the only woman whose loss had ever mattered. Fifteen years without hearing her voice or her laughter. Her magic had gone and the world was a darker place without her. Literally.

She stood there in the doorway without speaking.

"Aren't you going to bid me enter?"

"Stop talking like that. No. Go away." She tried to close the door on him but he blocked it with his foot.

"I need to talk to you, Sa'Rhea. Please."

"Don't call me that. I'm Rhea Harris now." She spoke low and looked out past him, making sure no one had overheard the exchange.

"Who is it? Oh shit..." Sarai came to a halt when she caught sight of Jaac. In the stillness of the moment, Rhea took him in. He was the mirror opposite of his brother. Dark where Paul had been fair, tall and broad where Paul had been thin and athletic. Deep eyes as dark as midnight stared back at her.

"He was just leaving," Rhea hissed.

"No he wasn't." Sarai pushed past Rhea. Grabbing his arm, she yanked him into the apartment and closed the door, locking it. "You can't ignore this, Rhea. What are you doing here, Jaac?"

"The Nameless. It's back and the entire western shore has fallen. We need you, Sa'Rhea."

Shock, cold and hard, slammed into her. Shaking off the hand at her upper arm, she fell into a chair. "How many?"

"A lot." Jaac was quiet as he watched her reaction. Still so fucking beautiful that looking at her hurt his chest. And he'd thrown it away like a stupid boy.

"A lot? You still a scientist, Jaac? That's very astute of you. Precise. A lot."

The dry sarcasm in her voice surprised him. The Sa'Rhea he'd known had been sweet and joyful. "Ten thousand, four hundred and six. Is that better?"

She opened her eyes and that stormy blue-gray gaze held him fast. "Don't piss me off, beefy."

"Beefy?"

Sarai snickered.

"Look, Paul Bunyan, tell me what it is you were sent here to say. I have things to do."

Sarai really seemed to think that was funny and he resolved to look it up when he could. "We need your Talent. There are no high level Practitioners left. At least none who can hold the Nameless back."

"And you come crawling to me? After shaming me and sending me away like I was nothing? *Now* I'm worth speaking to, when you need me?"

"We could have used the scrolls but they're gone now."

Immediately, he regretted his words when she flinched as if he'd physically struck her.

"You're an asshole, Jaac. I can't believe I let you in here." Sarai's voice lowered into a growl and her face took on a more feline shape.

Damn it, a familiar minx in fury mode. Perfect.

"I'm sorry. Okay? I didn't mean it. I know you...I know you had no choice. I believe your account of what happened." Sighing, he splayed his fingers out before his body and then pulled them into fists. "It doesn't change the fact that we need you desperately. You're the last of your line. Your father is too old."

"And my sister, Emmia?" Once she could have said "sisters", but no longer. "Your sisters?"

"Your sister may be strong enough with the aid of the scrolls but without them..." He shrugged. "The power holding the Nameless back has been weakening for the last fifteen years. Many of those remaining have been sent away to the Eastern Mountains."

"Who sent you here?"

"The Council. We need you. Please."

"My father? Yours?"

He sighed, nodding. "Yes. Both. Your father would have come but he's not in the best of health. He's been using most of his energy to keep the boundary up. The coastal cities are in danger but the wards are holding. For now."

Rhea went to look out the sliding glass door at the ocean. She'd yearned to be with her own people for fifteen years. Wanted to hear the sound of the food sellers as they called out their afternoon bargains. Missed her mother's humming and her sisters' laughter, her brothers teasing each other. Not that her mother could laugh from her grave. She missed her Talent. She wanted to go home.

Sarai came to stand next to her. "You don't owe them anything."

"Not the Council, no. But the millions who are threatened now, how can I ignore that?"

"You can't, because you're you. Get a guarantee that the geas against you has been lifted. Make sure the family holdings due you as Paul's widow are awarded so you have a place to live after this is over. It's not greed, Rhea, it's common sense. You can't come back here, you're dying. There you can have your magic back and a living. Fuck the rest of them." Sarai said it quietly but Jaac heard anyway.

"You're dying?" The panic in his voice was obvious.

"Not from a sickness. The environment here drains me. I can't keep it all out without a severe bleed on my powers."

He wanted to touch her. Pull her into his arms and kiss the lips he dreamt of every night. "I can assure you your widow property. I have the paperwork with me. You've got enough of a settlement to live comfortably for the rest of your life. The geas was lifted when you agreed to leave, by the way. You're free to return."

Home. The mere thought of it took away the aches and pains of her day. If she lived alone with Sarai in her home—even if no one ever spoke to her—it would be better than dying a universe away. And she'd be able to save millions of lives and Practice again.

"I have to call my employers here and then we can go."

Why an electronic book?

We live in the Information Age—an exciting time in the history of human civilization, in which technology rules supreme and continues to progress in leaps and bounds every minute of every day. For a multitude of reasons, more and more avid literary fans are opting to purchase e-books instead of paper books. The question from those not yet initiated into the world of electronic reading is simply: *Why?*

1. *Price.* An electronic title at Ellora's Cave Publishing and Cerridwen Press runs anywhere from 40% to 75% less than the cover price of the exact same title in paperback format. Why? Basic mathematics and cost. It is less expensive to publish an e-book (no paper and printing, no warehousing and shipping) than it is to publish a paperback, so the savings are passed along to the consumer.

2. *Space.* Running out of room in your house for your books? That is one worry you will never have with electronic books. For a low one-time cost, you can purchase a handheld device specifically designed for e-reading. Many e-readers have large, convenient screens for viewing. Better yet, hundreds of titles can be stored within your new library—on a single microchip. There are a variety of e-readers from different manufacturers. You can also read e-books on your PC or laptop computer. (Please note that Ellora's Cave does not endorse any specific brands.

You can check our websites at www.ellorascave.com or www.cerridwenpress.com for information we make available to new consumers.)

3. *Mobility.* Because your new e-library consists of only a microchip within a small, easily transportable e-reader, your entire cache of books can be taken with you wherever you go.

4. *Personal Viewing Preferences.* Are the words you are currently reading too small? Too large? Too... ANNOYING? Paperback books cannot be modified according to personal preferences, but e-books can.

5. *Instant Gratification.* Is it the middle of the night and all the bookstores near you are closed? Are you tired of waiting days, sometimes weeks, for bookstores to ship the novels you bought? Ellora's Cave Publishing sells instantaneous downloads twenty-four hours a day, seven days a week, every day of the year. Our webstore is never closed. Our e-book delivery system is 100% automated, meaning your order is filled as soon as you pay for it.

Those are a few of the top reasons why electronic books are replacing paperbacks for many avid readers.

As always, Ellora's Cave and Cerridwen Press welcome your questions and comments. We invite you to email us at Comments@ellorascave.com or write to us directly at Ellora's Cave Publishing Inc., 1056 Home Avenue, Akron, OH 44310-3502.

MAKE EACH DAY MORE *EXCITING* WITH OUR

ELLORA'S CAVEMEN

CALENDAR

☥ WWW.ELLORASCAVE.COM ☥

Discover for yourself why readers can't get enough
of the multiple award-winning publisher
Ellora's Cave.

Whether you prefer e-books or paperbacks,

be sure to visit EC on the web at
www.ellorascave.com

for an erotic reading experience that will leave you
breathless.